D1260599

WE ARE NOT ALONE

WE
ARE NOT
ALONE

BY

JAMES HILTON

LITTLE, BROWN AND COMPANY · BOSTON

Published March 1937
Reprinted March 1937

PR
6015
I 53W4

THE ATLANTIC MONTHLY PRESS BOOKS
ARE PUBLISHED BY
LITTLE, BROWN AND COMPANY
IN ASSOCIATION WITH
THE ATLANTIC MONTHLY COMPANY

WE ARE NOT ALONE

PROLOGUE

IN a small cathedral town where changes
are few, there are always people who remember who used to live in a particular house,
what happened to them there and afterwards,
and so on. Thus, when a chain-store company
bought a site at the corner of Shawgate and
sent men to break up the old Georgian frontage,
there were reminders all over the town —
"That was where the little doctor lived." It
was a long time ago. The house had never
been occupied since, and for a reason that made
passers-by stare curiously as the picks swung
through the dust clouds. In due course the
job reached a stage when the whole of an inside wall was exposed, and on it, still hanging,

3

a smashed picture which a workman sold for
half a crown to a bystander. It proved on examination to be a faded etching of angels
grouped around an arch of flowers, but when
viewed at more than arm's length the whole
design took on the likeness of a human skull.
Some forgotten Victorian artist must have
thought this clever; he could hardly have imagined that it would ever be so appropriate.

For the little doctor, who had lived in that
house for years, was finally hanged for the
murder of his wife. A young woman was
charged with him, and she too was sentenced
to death. The case attracted a good deal of
attention at the time, not only amongst the
general public but in legal circles also. "The
framing of the indictment to include both
prisoners," says one authority, "was perfectly
logical and proper, for English law holds that
if murder is committed, joint responsibility can
be established against any number of persons
without regard to the question of who struck
the fatal blow. Thus it was possible through-

out the Newcome trial to ignore the problem (interesting but perhaps insoluble) of individual behavior during the crucial hours. All the same, the defense seems to me to have been somewhat mismanaged; indeed, it was generally admitted afterwards that Sir Guy Lockhead made a cardinal mistake in putting Dr. Newcome in the witness box to face a Crown cross-examination. My own plan, had I been defending Newcome, would have been to stress the undoubted fact that all the evidence was circumstantial, and to urge that it was the duty of the prosecution to prove it to the hilt rather than expect my client to refute it. I am inclined to think that if this had been done, an opposite verdict might have been returned (even against the racial and political feeling that was aroused by the nationality of the female prisoner); for there was much in the doctor's favor had not his hesitations, inconsistencies, and far-fetched explanations created such a bad impression."

Thus one of the leading jurists of the day.

He was not present at the trial, nor is it likely that his balanced scrutiny would have been affected by the picture I have in my own mind, of a grey day, herald of winter, the gas jets in the courtroom dimmed and flickering, so that as daylight faded, the shapes of judge, jury, and prisoners swam in a greenish twilight: the muffled Cathedral chimes each quarter hour, the hissing of the heating apparatus, voices that droned on more and more slowly as if they must die at last in darkness.

The little doctor, as I saw him then, was very quiet and still. But once, during some evidence of a particularly repetitive kind, there came into his quietude a sudden emptying of consciousness that could only mean one thing, and that an extremely shocking thing in a man on trial for his life. *He had dozed off!* His head nodded for a moment, till a warder tapped him so vigorously on the shoulder that he nearly slid to the floor.

"The court would be obliged if the prisoner would pay attention."

6

"I beg your pardon," answered the little doctor, almost inaudibly.

If you were born in Calderbury during the first decade of the twentieth century, David Newcome may well have ushered you into the world, for he had begun to practise in 1899. A year after that he married the daughter of a rural dean; they had one child, a boy. Jessica mixed with the best Cathedral society and was always on the committee of this, that, and the other. David did n't share many of her interests; sometimes he went to Sunday service with her, but more often not, for a doctor has all the best excuses. He was generous, however, with subscriptions, and some of the Cathedral people called him "our doctor" because of his wife. Perhaps that was really why they also called him "little," since it was not he who was less than average in height, but Jessica who was more. She was five feet ten, which is tall enough in any woman.

Perhaps too there was endearment in the

7

diminutive, for a film of guilelessness often covered his brown eyes when he looked one over; and when he examined a child, one could think of two children examining each other. He had beautiful hands, simple manners (no manners at all, Jessica sometimes said), and a way of telling the truth if he thought you needed it. "There's nothing the matter with you," he would declare, quite simply, and leave you to try another doctor if you wanted coddling. His voice was quiet, and to those who preferred their own he would listen for a while — or, at any rate, seem to be listening. He smoked cherry-wood pipes which he bought for a penny each, and he always wore the same sort of dark blue suit. When he was seen about the town with Jessica people would say, acknowledging her by the adjective they bestowed on him, "There goes the little doctor."

Calderbury was a pleasant town in those days. I always thought it the right kind of place for civilized living — small enough to be walked through in half an hour, yet of a dignity and importance beyond mere size. Its Cathedral was good fourteenth-century Gothic with later accretions, and the only building of any rival conspicuousness was the massive stone jail, built in the thirties by an architect who took an evidently depressing view of the extent and permanence of Calderbury's criminality. The town itself, though you had heard of it, was probably one that you missed visiting thirty years ago, if only because the railway had sent it no more than the branch line of a branch line. Yet this was perhaps a lucky chance, for after half a century this line had come to easy terms with the town's prevalent mood, so that the time-table could conveniently dismiss the inquirer with a sentence: "See trains to Marsland and thence about five times daily."

Behind the streets rose the Knoll, a wooded hill surmounted by a stone obelisk; the best way to climb it was by the footpath from the steep part of Shawgate, beyond a row of Georgian houses. The little doctor lived in one of these. It was well-built and elegantly proportioned, but rather dark, owing to a cedar tree in the back garden and close-mesh curtains which, for front windows right on the street, were a needed barrier to the inquisitive. Calderbury folk were not more than normally curious, but the doctor's house stood halfway up the hill and most people climbed slowly, with halts to stare at shop windows, dogs in the gutter, or the butcher's boy freewheeling dangerously down. Assuredly the interior of Jessica's drawing-room, if visible, would have added to these attractions. It was very prim and chintzy, with water colors and illuminated mottoes and a model of a church, carved in sandalwood, which a missionary uncle had brought back from Ceylon.

Along the side of the house ran a narrow alley, flanked by rows of white shells, spoils from some unidentifiable seashore. These pointed the way to the doctor's surgery, which, at some earlier period of its existence, had been a lean-to greenhouse, so that a faintly horticultural atmosphere still clung to its shelving and glass roof, even though the former was crowded with bottles and the latter covered by adjustable paper blinds. It was, if you came to think about it, an exceedingly cramped, unsuitable, and ill-arranged structure, but it had, for David, the incomparable advantage of being a place apart.

Not that, in any conscious way, he had grown tired of Jessica. It was rather that his attitude towards her had leveled into a passive acceptance of her status as his wife; no flicker of impulse disturbed something which was not quite serenity and not quite boredom either. This condition, which some people flatteringly call happiness, David did not call anything; he did not even think about it. He just did his job, year by year, and would have been tolerably content with the wrong sort of wife if only he could have had the right sort of child. It did n't seem, as the years went by, that Gerald was going to be that. There was a nervousness in the boy that was almost pathological, and none the less so because Jessica regarded it as mere naughtiness. Upon this point of interpretation David and Jessica had their rare quarrels; for the boy's tantrums stirred David to a degree of patience which to Jessica was an added irritation. Curious foolery, so it was reported by those who had access to overlooking windows, went on in the Shawgate garden between father and son — foolery in which it would have been hard to say whose behavior was the more fantastically infantile. Jessica always thought the whole thing was rather disgraceful. But when Gerald developed one of his notorious crying fits it was David who would devote hours to pacifying him, fighting the enemy with fear-stilling hands; for David knew the terror a child can have when a shadow climbs a wall, or when a train screams through a station, or when, in some story book, a page is turned shudderingly upon a hated picture. And he knew how terror can sometimes fascinate till the dreaded thing is loved and the mind twists into lonely corridors; he knew, too, that nothing is terrible if it is not felt to be. For there was that picture of angels looking like a skull; by some chance the boy liked it, and was overjoyed when David produced a real skull — relic of student days — to give meaning to what had hitherto been a merely entertaining mystery. And David, demonstrating thus, was inspired to do so by an intrepidity he could hardly explain — a desire to establish one thing at least of which the boy should never be afraid; and that was Death.

David's practice was one of the best in Calderbury, but that was not so very good, and there was nothing sensational about it — thousands of small-town doctors followed a similar routine. The brass plate said "Physician and Surgeon," and of these functions the latter consisted of emergency work and operations on his own patients at their homes or in the local hospital. In those days there was less specialization and more all-round versatility; David could clip off an appendix or chisel a mastoid with as much confidence as he would invade territory now held by the dentist and the chiropodist. He was, indeed, an excellent surgeon and there was a sense, difficult for the layman not to misinterpret, in which he *enjoyed* a morning at the operating table. Physicking was the more arduous, since it entailed a daily tour of Calderbury's narrow streets, the climbing of innumerable dark and steep stairways, and — every evening except Sunday — a two-hour session in the surgery.

You did not, unless you belonged to Cathedral society, make a special appointment to see the little doctor. If you were well enough you came, you waited, and you were seen. And if, unfortunately, you were n't well enough, then a familiar phenomenon turned the corner of the street — the little doctor on a very shabby bicycle, with his bag strapped to a carrier over the rear mudguard. The streets of Calderbury were mostly steep and cobbled, and he rode along them with a degree of peril well orchestrated by experience. He always said that he could n't afford to motor, and when it was suggested that he could, he fell back on a second line of defense by saying that cycling gave him hard exercise and that otherwise he would have none. But the truth was probably that he disliked changes and found it hard to make up his mind for them. So he went on cycling throughout the year, in rain and cold winds and fog; and one day in 1910, after a crash into the back of a farm cart on Lissington Hill, it was wondered amongst Calderbury citizens whether he would buy a car at last. But no; he bought another bicycle. And he had, by the way, a peculiar style of mounting and dismounting: he would wheel the machine a few paces, stare at it intensely for a second or two, and then, with an extraordinary upward and sideways leap, launch himself on to the saddle by means of a projecting "step" on the back axle. I never saw another cyclist do anything like it, and I do not know whether the little doctor was ever taught it in those far-off nineties when people *were* taught cycling, or whether he invented it himself.

He was well liked in Calderbury. He did not waste much time in spoken sympathy, or even seem to worry much if his patients died, though he was sometimes inclined to boast if they did n't die — as when, for instance, in an epidemic that killed scores of other doctors' patients, all of his recovered. He spoke of it as if it were some unique athletic feat of his own that deserved a trophy. But this boasting was only juvenile and superficial. Actually he was no more appalled by death than by life — he had seen it too often, and knew from what agonies it could bring release. He had, quite unsentimentally, a sense of human fellowship that passed beyond tearful bedside faces to the sublime muteness of suffering — contact compared with which mere personal grief was exhibitionism. And there was something more, a sense of the sheer awfulness of physical existence that gave him sympathy with every whimpering child, yet also, remotely, with the ills he had to combat, so that he could muse upon the progress of a disease as he might upon

the quickening of spring in his own back
garden.

A large map of England hung on the wall of
the surgery waiting room; Cornwall was yellow, Devon red, Hampshire cream, and you
couldn't tell the difference between Cumber-
land and Westmoreland because they were so
far away at the top. There was an oblong
mahogany table with nothing on it but a plant-
less plant pot and some tattered magazines.
On the mantelpiece a gilt clock ticked loudly
under a glass dome, and above this hung a
framed diploma certifying in a very spidery
handwriting something that nobody ever bothered to stand on a chair and read. Fifteen
chairs, in fact, were ranged against the four
walls, and when they were all occupied the
assembly, with the big table in the middle,
looked like some fantastic board meeting. You
had time to notice all these things while waiting for your turn. And at intervals the inner
glass-paneled door would open, a patient would
emerge and the next one rise eagerly; and then

you would hear two distinctive good-evenings: the one that meant "You're calmer now, you can go away easier in mind; things are n't quite so bad, are they?" — and the other that meant "You're worried, I know. Please tell me all about it; I'm here to help you." And when, on summer nights, the sunlight slanted in, you could watch the yellow bars climb up from the Isle of Wight to Birmingham — never higher because of the roof across the street; and after they had gone away altogether Susan would come in with a lighted taper for the gas. It burned green and pale, with a hissing sound. And then the inner door opening again. . . . "Good evening" — "Good evening. . . ." Oh, little doctor, please be kind to me when it comes my turn. . . .

So, as a child, one watched and prayed while the Cathedral bells chimed the quarters; and the prayer was answered. He was kind, none ever kinder. Once, when he had pulled out a loose tooth not quite painlessly, he promised a child a real steam engine with real steam. It was absurd, since it would cost far more than the fee, and no one expected anything to come of it — no one except the child, who believed and waited in vain. But a story came from the man who kept the town's toy shop — that David had been there to buy the steam engine, but that Jessica interfered and would n't let him spend the money. One could hardly blame her.

The trouble with genius (because I think, in some ways, there was a touch of that quality in the little doctor) is that it is essentially alone. The most you know is that it is there; you cannot really come to terms with it; it is something that gives and cannot take. There were times when David sat by the bedside of old and dying people, and something passed between them in a finger touch; but you could no more describe it or analyze it than you can trap the wisp of memory that strays from a forgotten dream. And it came again in his jokes with children. Most of these look rather silly on paper, but here is one which was remembered because it shocked Jessica so much. There were mice in the kitchen of the house and she had sent for Tom Riddle, who was Calderbury's vermin catcher and insect exterminator — a friendly little fellow with a drooping moustache and a squeaky voice. It so happened that he arrived in the midst of a children's party and announced himself as "the mice man." This seemed to amuse David enormously and he began a sort of game with the children to find how many other kinds of men would rhyme with "mice man" — "rice man, ice man, nice man," and so on. Whereupon Teddy Farrell suggested "Christ man" (he was the seven-year-old son of the Archdeacon and had probably caught the phrase from one of his father's sermons), and David, laughing like a child himself, began to make a jingle of it: —

> Mice man or Christ man,
> So long as you're a nice man —

but Jessica would n't let him get any further. She thought it was blasphemous, and even more urgently wondered what Teddy would go home and tell his father.

I daresay I was too old, when I first met him, ever to know the little doctor in this childlike and more elemental sense. I was twelve and had for years suffered from recurring bouts of asthma. Other doctors had grown tired of me; patent medicines had been tried in vain. So I went at last to David, and it was then, one summer evening, that I watched the sunlight climb the counties over the map. When my turn came I sat in the leather armchair that had a footrest and a swivel arrangement for tilting backwards, and described (as clearly as only a bright grammar-school boy can) exactly what was the matter with me. Was it very serious? Would I ever get better? Was there a cure?

"I don't really know," David said (it was one of the things which a doctor should never say and which David often said), and after looking puzzled for a moment added: "But I think you ought to keep a diary."

"I *do*," I answered, rather proudly.

"And do you put in it everywhere you go every day?"

"Yes."

"Well, you must go on doing that, and you must also put down how the asthma is every day. . . . Do you like detective stories?"

I said I did, and he lent me *Trent's Last Case.*

For two months I kept that diary, noting each day where I went and how much better or worse I was. Then I went to see him again. "Ah," he said, "now we can behave as if we were from Scotland Yard. A crime has been committed and we must look for clues. I see that on April nineteenth, after visiting your Uncle Richard, you had a particularly bad attack. Now what's your hypothesis?"

That was just how a boy of twelve, and top of his class, liked to be talked to; and in less than a week a theory was formulated. Just *cats.* Uncle Richard had a cat, and so had other people whom I knew and visited; I liked cats and always fondled them at every opportunity. But David was n't satisfied till he had taken me to Chancey Gardens.

Chancey was a place about fifty miles away where there were, and perhaps still are, side shows, a small zoo, and an amusement park. The expedition required a whole day, and it seemed remarkable, to others much more than to me, that David should hand over his affairs to a colleague in order to give a schoolboy an outing. But we had a good time. We tried the merry-go-round and the test-your-strength machines, and afterwards we ate ice cream out of penny cones. Then we looked in at the lion house, where I promptly began to sneeze and gasp for breath. "You see?" David said, quite pleased with himself. *"Any* of the cat tribe, apparently . . . now that 's *very* remarkable. . . ."

So I avoided the cat tribe, and the asthma left me. Whenever I met David again he would ask me how I was, but I felt that he already half-knew and was for that reason less interested. I always hoped he would take me somewhere again (in fact I used to dream he would), but he never did, and our trip to Chancey became a strange memory in the end. Because I loved the little doctor, and it was because of me, partly, that he was hanged.

CHAPTER I

ONE cold gusty night in December a boy rang the bell of the doctor's house in Shawgate, and when Susan came to the door left word that there had been an accident to a dancer at the local theatre and would the doctor please come at once. Bestowing her usual skeptical scrutiny on such a messenger, Susan pressed for further details, but the boy could give none and ran off home, leaving her to waken David from the peacefulness of a last pipe in the surgery. He had had a busy day and was tired, but when she reported the message he nodded vaguely and began putting things in his bag.

"At the theatre, Susan? A dancer?"

"So the boy said. I don't know why they should send for you, anyway — Dr. Cowell lives much nearer."

"I 'd better go."

"It 's probably nothing much. Shall I light your bicycle lamp for you?"

"Oh, I think I 'll walk. It 's only over the hill past the Cathedral."

"But it 's a rough night."

"Do me good to get some fresh air. I can walk it in ten minutes."

He put on his overcoat, wrapped a muffler round his neck, pulled the brim of his hat well down, and set out. He often walked if his destination were near the Cathedral, for the steepness of Shawgate made cycling hardly worth while. Besides, for a late evening call, it was a good way of waking up. Many times on similar occasions he had conquered the inertia of the body, moving in sheer automatism through the dark streets until physical effort or mental curiosity provoked a liveliness. And if anyone had said there was anything especially fine in such self-discipline, he would have answered that it was just a job, and that no one hated it sometimes more than he.

A rough night, indeed. There were few strollers in such weather, and the Cathedral, chiming the hour of ten, seemed to bowl the strokes along the corridors of the wind. It was one of those nights when, in imagination, the centuries slipped back and Calderbury was again a fortress of souls with a priestly garrison; every lighted window hinting at safety amidst peril, the warm, tranquil comfort of men who felt they were safe because they knew they were saved. Such an atmosphere had lingered from the age of Chaucer to the age of Dickens, and though modernity might seem to efface it in the daytime, there only needed a dark night for its return. It harbored, too, a feeling that earth and stones could hold some secret essence of all that had happened around and about them, so that after a thousand years a street became almost animate, leaning its walls a little forward to catch the sound of friendly footsteps. David

felt that his own footsteps *were* friendly, both
to past and to present; that he was a part of
the continuous agony of existence that had
clustered about this ancient hill since the first
mason carved the first gargoyle. And even
longer; for the whole span of centuries from
cathedral to cinema was but a scratch upon the
heritage of a million weather-beaten years.

So he mused (being slightly pagan and
pantheist as well as Christian, and slightly ag-
nostic about all of it) as he turned the angle
whence Shawgate makes its steeper aim direct
to the Cathedral towers. And because he was
tired and a little breathless from climbing
against the gale, he halted a moment by a
street lamp; and again because there was a
playbill of the local theatre in a shop window
near by, he crossed the pavement to give it a
second's glance.

It advertised a show called *Les Nuit* [*sic*] *de
Paris,* which it described as "A Riot of Mirth-
Provoking Naughtiness, Direct from the Gay
Capital, with a Galaxy of Continental Stars."

The Theatre Royal in Calderbury dated
from the fifties and had been modernized at
various times to conform with fashions that
afterwards made it seem more outmoded than
ever; in structure it was the type that Crummles
had played in, with horseshoe auditorium and
a long-disused and very lofty "gods." In its
day it had ministered to the cream as well as
to the milk of Calderbury society — even clerics
had occupied its uncomfortable red plush seats
to watch Mrs. Ebbsmith push her Bible into
the fire, or to see Boucicault's Colleen Bawn
dive into a tank of real water and come up
dripping to take a curtain call. Which, of
course, was somewhat before the little doctor
came to Calderbury, and a good deal before the
first picture camera flickered in a converted
mission hall off Briargate. By the time of *Les
Nuit* [*sic*] *de Paris* the theatre had sunk to a
level from which not even clerical visitation
could or would effect a rescue. Stucco had
peeled off the outside walls, the words "Theatre Royal" were spelt in empty sockets for

which nobody could afford lights, moth and fleas inhabited the plush-hung boxes that nobody ever entered. The very boards of the stage sagged with dry rot, which was, indeed, the cause of mishap during the third act of one of those Parisian nights.

That third and last act was nearly over when David arrived. He found nobody on duty to admit or question him. Entering by the stage door, he made his way along a dimly lit corridor echoing with the sound of excessively nasal singing. Then he pushed through another door and found himself stumbling against a heap of bright-colored dresses. Here a stout man in shirt sleeves seemed to be manipulating scenery.

"I 've been sent for — " began David.

"Just a minute," answered the stout man, suddenly hauling till the veins of his forehead stood out; whereat the singing swelled into climactic frenzy, whistling and shouting answered it, and a moment later an avalanche of girls swept past the little doctor as he waited, bag in hand. They chattered together, some rough-voiced and crudely spoken, a few round-shouldered and flat-chested; one girl coughed and clung momentarily to an iron pillar; another stopped to scratch herself. It was a new atmosphere for him, but full of pathological landmarks, signals of flesh and blood which stood, so many of them, at danger. The girls shed their skirts to make another heap of clothes, and from this, as from some multi-petaled flower, there rose a mingled smell of dust, cheap perfume, old wood, and human bodies.

"I'm a doctor. Someone sent for me about an accident here."

The stout man turned a casual eye. "Accident?" Then, into space: "Hey, Jim! Know anything about an accident?"

"To one of your dancers," David added, recollecting.

A voice answered: "We ain't got only one dancer. She slipped as she came off, if you call that an accident."

31

The stout man jerked his hand. "Maybe it's her. You'll find her along there."

"Thank you."

David walked between cliffs of slowly swaying canvas till he came to a group of girls wiping grease paint from their faces. They took no notice of him and after a moment he asked: "Is there a girl here who dances?"

"Oh, you mean What's-her-name? Try the door right at the end."

He walked farther till a closed door stopped him; he tapped on the panel, but there was no answer; then he turned the handle and found the room empty. He went back to the girls.

"There's nobody in."

"No? Then she must have gone home."

"But — well, I'm a doctor — I was sent for to see this girl — or to see someone, at any rate — about an accident."

"An accident?"

"Hasn't there been an accident? Didn't she slip and hurt herself?"

32

"Don't know, I'm sure. We weren't on during her turn."

Had they been less casual, had they been able to confirm or deny or explain anything, he would probably have concluded that since the girl had been well enough to go home she could not have been very badly hurt. And he would probably have gone home then himself, assuming his summons to have been a thing done hastily and afterwards regretted. But that air of casualness, so foreign to the routine of his own profession, stiffened his conscientiousness to the point of obstinacy; even if the whole thing were a hoax or a false alarm, he could not now be satisfied till he had definitely established it so. After some trouble he extracted the girl's temporary address from the stage doorkeeper: Number 24, Harcourt Row.

He walked there in a drizzling mist; the wind had calmed suddenly, and the bare trees hung tired and still and heavy with raindrops. One might have noticed then that he wasn't really little at all, merely that his well-proportioned figure marked a difference from the common identification of size and strength. There was something resolute in his stride along the pavements, and a look of quiet challenge in the way he turned the corner of the Row and glanced up at the dark façade.

At Number 24 an elderly woman answered his continued ringing; she had to unlock the door. He knew her by sight; she knew him in the same way; and only this prevented the voicing of her resentment at being dragged out of bed at such an hour. Even as it was, her manner was far from cordial. When David had stated his business she muttered truculently: "Well, so far as I know she's in bed and asleep by now. She had her key. I never wait up. It's bad enough to let to theatricals without having to keep their hours."

"Is that her room immediately above the porch?"

"Yes, that's it."

"There's a light in the window."

"And I suppose you want me to see if anything's the matter?"

"Just find out if she sent for me, that's all. You see, *somebody* sent for me."

"It would n't be the first time they've hoaxed a doctor," she retorted, as she shuffled along in her slippers and began to climb the stairs. David remained in the dark hallway, trying to recall her name — ah yes, she was Mrs. Patterson; her husband had been Joe Patterson — worked at the brewery — diabetic — died of it — one of Cowell's patients. A doctor remembers things that way. He could hear the creak of the joists as Mrs. Patterson walked over them, the sound of a door opening; he could smell stale cooking and stuffy rooms. He had waited in so many houses, had climbed so many stairs to so many bedrooms, that his nerves as well as his ears and eyes and nostrils had acquired a curious sensitivity to the atmosphere of an interior; and now, waiting in that small lodging house in Harcourt Row, awareness came to him of something strange and unusual. He had no time to wonder what it was, or even whether it had any existence outside his own mood; for Mrs. Patterson creaked her way down the stairs carrying a lighted candle.

"You'd better come up and see her. I can't understand a word she says — she's foreign. She's hurt her arm, by the look of it."

"All right."

He followed upstairs, till the woman opened the door of a very small room, crowded with shabby furniture and lit by a single unshaded gas light. A bed occupied most of the space, and on this sat a girl. David saw her face first of all through a wall mirror that happened to be in line with it; stained with grease paint, it struck him disturbingly, so that he stared for a moment, hardly realizing that the eyes he met in the glass could really be seeing him also.

They were amber-brown, curiously matched with reddish-tinted hair; matched, too, in their pained, difficult eagerness, with the set of lips and mouth. David went to her. He saw at

36

once that her left wrist, resting over her knee as she sat, hung limply. She did not speak, but pointed to it, and when he stooped and held it, feeling what was amiss, her lips parted and blood came rushing into the marks that her teeth had made.

"It is brokken?" she said.

"I'm afraid so," he answered simply, kneeling to open his bag on a chair. He noticed then that a piece of stocking stuck to her leg in a smear of blood and dirt; nothing much, but the kind of thing he was always careful about. After bandaging the wrist he set about to clean this cut and asked Mrs. Patterson for warm water.

"You're going to have to rest for a while," he said to the girl.

She nodded, but he was not sure that she knew what he meant.

"You dance, don't you?"

Again she nodded.

"Well, you'll have to rest. You can't dance with an arm in a sling, and that's what you'll

37

have to have." He spoke plainly, as he always did, but with compassion and increasing doubt as to whether she understood him. "You know *some* English?" he queried.

"Ein wenig . . . a little. . . ."

He smiled more easily. "That's about how much I speak your language, too."

He was prepared then for the torrent of words that usually outpours if one confesses even a slight knowledge of a stranger's tongue; but to his surprise she was silent.

He tried to make conversation but soon came to the end of his scantily recollected German. He had never been in Germany or spoken the language colloquially; and it was fully fifteen years ago that he had studied it for some very elementary examination. Since then he would lazily have accepted the statement that he "knew German," but now, on such sudden demand, he found he could not remember equivalents for even the commonest words. And her own meagre English did nothing to help him out. But he did manage to ask why she had n't

38

waited for him at the theatre, since she had sent for him there.

"I did n't send for you," she answered, in German. "It was the boy who sells chocolates. He sent for you. He said you were always so very kind."

David was just as embarrassed as most men would be by such a remark.

She went on: "He called you 'the little doctor' — is that right? . . . *'Der kleine Doktor?'* "

Which completed his embarrassment, for he was one of those people who can live a whole lifetime without seeing or hearing the most obvious thing about themselves. He had not really known that he was called "the little doctor" until that moment, and he did not quite know whether he liked it or not; and, anyhow, the disclosure left him shyly disconcerted. And beyond all that he was troubled, perhaps by the rescoring of ancient mind tracks that the translation effort had entailed. He kept smiling the more steadfastly because he had used up all his German, and into a silence, as he packed his bag to go, came a revelation of her own mute solitariness in suffering. This made him feel towards her as to all such sufferers — that nothing could ever ease the embrace of pain and its victim except a gentle blessing on that embrace; and such a blessing he gave, in secret, on her behalf.

"Good night," he said, adding that he would call and see her again on Monday morning.

On the way back to his house it occurred to him that he did not even know her name. He stopped again at the shop window and glanced down at the playbill till he came to "Leni Arkadrevna, Whirlwind Danseuse from St. Petersburg." Goodness, he thought; that must be the one!

On Monday, when he called, the girl had left. "She just went off yesterday morning, same as the theatricals always do of a Sunday."

"But she had a broken wrist! She could n't be any use like that!"

"Well, maybe she had to go with the rest of 'em. Not that they seemed to have much to do with her, and you can't hardly blame them, with her not speaking the language."

"But were n't there other foreigners in the company? Was n't it a French play?"

"Bless you, they was all English except her. And the show's not really foreign — it's just what they call it to make it sound better. She acted a Russian dancer, so I suppose that's why they gave her the name."

"It was n't her real name, then?"

"Should n't think so. They never have real names."

"Do you know where the company's moved on to?"

"That I could n't say for sure, but I 've an idea it might be Addington or Polesby or one of them places. They 'd tell you at the theatre, I daresay."

But David did n't bother to ask at the theatre. His curiosity was soon exhausted, for the theatrical world had seemed so unfamiliar when

41

he had entered it momentarily that he could now accept any strangeness in its behavior. He was not passionately interested in the way touring companies functioned. Nor did he often think about the Russian-German-French girl (or whatever she really was) during the weeks that followed. He supposed she must be getting on all right somewhere or other; but it was n't his business, and he had too much other business, to inquire. He did n't even put her down in his book, because he had forgotten her stage name, and, anyhow, he was n't going to send in a bill. And this was not wholly generosity, but partly mere trouble saving; for he had no secretary, and the extraction of small sums from patients who left the town was rarely worth the time and effort it would involve.

CHAPTER II

THE New Year came in, and life for the little doctor continued pretty much as it had throughout a number of old years; busily partitioned, and with its own private trouble (about Gerald) to fill the gaps between; a dull life if one could not guess the interest in his job that solely sustained him. He did not talk much about that job; he did not even have time to think about it, in an abstract sense, save when he was alone. Then his work would acquire a totality in which separate items might be puzzled over like a problem, but never ached over like a worry.

He did not have many free moments. Most of his day was occupied with hospital work or visiting, he took his meals with Jessica, and in the evening there was the surgery; after which he was often tired enough to go to bed and very promptly to sleep.

Once a week, varying the routine, he spent a whole day in Sandmouth. He had several patients in that rising watering place — Calderbury folk who, retired and rich, lengthened their lives by means of sea air, half-yearly dividends, and (he always hoped) the confidence they reposed in his own regular visits. He was inclined to smile at this confidence (since there were so many excellent doctors in Sandmouth); nevertheless, he enjoyed his day trips to the sea. He took few definite holidays, and if he did, he and Jessica and Gerald went away for a fortnight, which was much longer than he cared to be idle. But the Sandmouth excursions were pleasantly enforced by his work; he did not add that he liked them all the more because he made them by himself.

They happened on Fridays, as a rule, and began by a morning cup of tea in the surgery long before anyone else in the house was astir; then came the walk to the station up the hill, through the Cathedral Close, and down the hill the other side. He liked that walk. It was a different life that one saw before seven in the morning — an hour at which all good deans and archdeacons were asleep, but at which in wintertime the lights were burning in innumerable little houses, workmen were washing over kitchen sinks, and their wives frizzling bacon and poking fires that had been banked down the night before. The working-class population of Calderbury was larger than a visitor might have suspected; indeed, within a few hundred yards of the Cathedral, in houses picturesquely ivy-clad, were conditions of overcrowding as deplorable as any in the more notorious slums of the big cities. David knew this. Presumably the Cathedral authorities knew it also, since they owned the property.

One summer morning he caught, as usual, the seven-five — an absurdly early train, but

45

there was no other till afternoon, and in those days travelers were at the mercy of the railway schedule. (To-day the buses leave for Sand-mouth every hour from Calderbury Market Square, and do the journey, without change, in seventy minutes.) But the doctor did not mind the two and a half hours of starts and stops, of chuff-chuffing through the dappled countryside, with the tang of sea in the air for the last twenty miles. It gave him a chance to read the paper and a detective novel, to talk to some casually met stranger, to smoke his pipe, and (as a last resort) to do nothing at all but sit back and think. That girl of Mrs. Pembar's — was it a blood dyscrasia or just an abnormal sensitivity? And old Doubleday's self-styled "rheumatics," which was really osteo-arthritis and would kill him in the end, what was to be done — was there anything that could be done? For that matter his own son . . . Mysterious flesh and bones and juices — so sweet for pleasure, so sour for pain; prison of man and empire to microbe; but beyond all that, as in

46

Gerald, the dark alchemy of the mind that no brain surgery could explore. It was a problem that always beguiled him, and one to which, had he been granted time and the chance to specialize, he would have devoted himself. But his approach to it was, for those days, eccentric; he believed that mind was more than physical brain, and different from it in character — something that neither the surgeon's knife nor the analyst's reagents could reveal. He felt that it was, in a sense, pure God-stuff, and that the treatment of mental disease must leave the sphere of physical things and become spiritual, even mystic. The staff at Midchester County Asylum, of which he was on the Board and which he visited regularly, chaffed him about this and called him "the Witch Doctor," and he chaffed them back by saying that it was a title he would gladly accept, and would they please appoint him officially?

In Sandmouth that Friday morning the June sun blazed in a manner almost justifying the

railway posters, and Station Avenue, sloping
down to the Pierhead, was brilliant with the
litter of café advertisements and stalls piled
with colored buckets and gift pottery. Trams
heaved over loops, while down every side street
boarding-house maids breathed in the far-
famed Sandmouth ozone through the dust and
smells of their basement areas. David walked
briskly along pavements jammed with children
sucking sticks of "rock" and grown-ups
dawdling with precautionary mackintoshes;
then he turned the corner by the Pierhead and
threaded his way along the Promenade. Here
the main army of holiday-makers paraded,
beach photographers touted for custom, and the
wire cages attached to lampposts filled up with
banana skins and chocolate wrappings as fast
as Corporation scavengers could empty them.
Sandmouth on a summer day was not a
wholly beautiful sight, but it was always
human enough to be abundantly interesting, and when the weather was good
David liked to walk by the edge of the waves,

noticing the faces of deck-chair loungers and stumbling over sand holes dug by frantic children.

That morning the sea was warm and calm, but the sky had a watery brightness foretelling clouds which, soon after midday, threw down spots of rain. It was during the afternoon that he made his visits; they were usually finished by five, so that he could comfortably catch the five-thirty. But the call at Mrs. Drawbell's lengthened because a niece staying with her had taken a chill, and the call at Major Sanderson's lengthened because the Major insisted on describing a new kind of indigestion he had acquired — to which David listened with sympathy combined with growing apprehension about the time. In the end he reconciled himself to losing the train, though actually, had he hurried, he could have caught it. He was like that — he would rather decide to miss something than have the uncertainty of chasing after it. There was no other train till the nine-seven, so he had three hours to spare. He strolled

49

down Station Avenue to the Promenade where grey skies were breaking into one of those spectacular sea-horizon sunsets which can only be likened to picture-postcard views of themselves which would never attract the discriminating purchaser. The air, however, was cool and full of fragrances lifted by the rain, and now that the evening promised to be fine the crowds were beginning to emerge from hotels and boarding houses. David reached the Pierhead and, on sudden impulse, paid his twopence and clicked on to the wooden planks. There was something in the sound of walking on them, and in the splash of waves below, that gave him memories too far and strange to be analyzed; he had not been on Sandmouth Pier for years. It was a quarter of a mile long, terminating in a pavilion in which summer concert parties gave twice-nightly performances. One of these was imminent as he neared the festoons of colored electric globes that marked the pavilion entrance, and for a moment he watched the audience trickling in twos and

threes past the pay booth. He noticed that the
concert party advertised themselves as "The
Cheerybles"; presently, approaching a placard
more closely than before, his eye caught a programme announcement. One of its items en-
gaged something in his mind that made him
pause. "Leni Arkadrevna," he reread, "Whirlwind Danseuse from St. Petersburg." Then
he remembered, and on a second sudden impulse that evening he turned to the pay booth
and bought a shilling deck-chair seat facing
the open-air stage. The show was just beginning.

He did not find it very entertaining, but a
certain innocent curiosity about most things
made it hard for him to feel bored; indeed, as
he watched and listened to the rather feeble acting and singing, a slow dreamy contentment
came over him, focused slightly by the anticipation of seeing his ex-patient again. At any
rate, with the alternative of nothing else to do,
he did not regret the whim that had brought
him to such a place. He enjoyed awareness of

the massed humanity around him and of the
snaky sea underneath — a hint of peril in such
an assembly.   And he was amused by a young
man with an attractive smile who came jauntily
forward and sang a song with words something
like: —

> "Poor old England is n't in the picture,
>   Everything is foreign, you 'll agree,
> The table and the chairs,
> The carpet on the stairs,
>   Were made in Ger-man-ee!
> But when you go out into the garden,
>   Nestling in a little plot,
> There 's the sweetest English rose
> That in the summer grows,
>   And that 's the only bit of English
>   that we 've got!"

A piquant prelude to the appearance of a whirlwind dancer from St. Petersburg who spoke
German.   But, to his surprise, she did n't ap-
pear, and her item on the programme was
omitted without explanation; till suddenly,
from the unison with which a particular chorus

was sung, he realized that the show was over and the audience beginning to get up and move away. After a pause he rose with them and sauntered towards the exit, puzzled, but hardly troubling much. When, however, he passed a man in Pierrot costume who was about to enter the pay booth, he asked what had happened to the girl dancer. The question ignited something.

"Happened to her? You can well ask that!"

"Why, what's the matter?"

Just then another Pierrot rushed up and said something in the ear of the first one, whose response was to throw up his arms with a gesture of despair. "My God — she *would!* And now what do we do? A doctor — where the devil can we find a doctor?"

"I am a doctor," said David quietly.

"You?"

"Yes."

"No kidding?"

"My name is — "

53

"Oh, never mind — for heaven's sake go round and see what's up. Take him along, Jim."

Jim led the way through the rows of empty deck chairs, now awaiting their second audience, behind a wooden screen, and eventually to the back of the stage. It was part of David's experience to be guided by devious routes to strange places, there to take charge of emergencies that occasioned him no real surprise. Only the mildest curiosity inspired him to ask his question again — what had happened to the girl? Was she ill?

"It's only luck if she isn't dead."

"Oh?"

"Shut herself in and turned on the gas, mister. What d' you say to that?"

But all David could say to that was a rather surprised: "Gas on the end of a pier?"

"Yes, mister. Gas an' electric light and water and telephone — all in them pipes. You wouldn't think it, would you?"

Soon they came upon an excited group of

54

concert artists and Pier officials. Someone was fanning a door backwards and forwards, and there was much eagerness to describe, rather confusingly, what had taken place. The girl, it seemed, had missed her cue for the whirlwind dance business, and nobody had had time to find out the reason for her absence until after the last curtain, when a locked door and a smell of gas were discovered and reported. The door was easily opened with the key of another door; then the girl was found, sprawled over a couch, half-dressed in the costume of her act, unconscious and breathing heavily in the tainted atmosphere. The tap of the radiator had been full on.

David took in the scene professionally, noting the absence of skin discoloration and the comparative steadiness of the pulse. But most of all he noticed that her injured wrist, the one he had attended in Calderbury six months before, was badly swollen.

There came over him at these times a sort of natural dignity, so that when he asked the crowd to disperse and leave him alone in the room, they did so without much demur.

"Nothing to be alarmed about," he said, reassuringly.

"You mean she'll pull through?" queried a thin man in evening clothes.

"Yes, she'll be all right soon."

"You really think so?"

"Why, of course." And he added, almost as if he were speaking to himself: "These walls are only matchboarding — they're full of draughts. I don't think anybody could do such a thing here without stopping up the cracks . . . it's extraordinary, the way people don't think of these details. . . ."

"Well, there's one detail you can think of to save me the trouble, doctor."

"Yes?"

"As soon as she comes to you can tell her she's got the sack."

David looked up inquiringly.

"I'm the manager and I don't stand for this sort of thing. So you can tell her — see?"

David was still looking up.

"And tell her to clear out before we fetch the police! She could be locked up for this!"

"I wouldn't fetch the police if I were you," said David quietly. "It wouldn't do your show any good."

The manager banged the door, and David began — artificial respiration, a hypodermic, just the routine procedure. He went to work with his usual precision, yet with something more than his usual awareness of irrelevancies: the little wooden dressing room, even shabbier than the brick one at Calderbury; the spotted mirror; the litter of paints and powders in front of it; an out-of-date trade calendar hanging on the wall; and — after a little while — the sound of piano and voices striking up the opening chorus of the second show. Odd background, odd accompaniment. And since it is often the oddest things that are apt to move one, so, as he looked at her, noting the closed eyes, the slightly parted lips, and the rise and fall of the breath, what touched him most to

57

pity were the soles of her bare feet, hunched under her as she lay, and dirty from contact with the unswept floor boards.

Presently she opened her eyes. They blinked to consciousness as she realized where she was, then focused to new astonishment at the sight of him; while her mouth, trying the German words before she spoke, twisted into a half-smile.

"*You?* I must be dreaming! How can it be *you — here?*"

And he answered, with the foolishness of sheer simplicity: "I come here every Friday."

"*Der kleine Doktor am jeden Freitag!*"

He sat beside her, rebandaging the wrist, trying to think of German words.

"You must take care. This is bad. . . . Am I hurting you now?"

"Only a little."

"You should have rested — I told you that. . . ."

"I could n't."

"You mean you danced with your wrist in this condition?"

"Yes — until to-night."

"But it must have been terribly painful — the vibration — "

"It was driving me mad."

"But, my dear girl — why on earth — why — was *that* why — you tried to — "

She shook her head.

"Then why?"

"Just — that there was nothing else."

"Nichts anders?"

"Nothing except night after night — like this."

"Could n't you go back to your own country?"

She shook her head again.

"You have no parents there — no relatives — no friends?"

"No one."

"Is that why you are unhappy?"

All at once tears began to roll down her cheeks, streaking the grease paint; she did not make a sound, and there was no movement but that of the tears. Neither did David move, but his stillness and silence had compassion.

After a pause she smiled. He asked the reason and took to his heart a schoolboy translation of her answer: "Because I am so glad you did n't tell me not to cry . . . and I knew you would n't. . . ."

A doctor is so familiar with most of the things that can happen to minds and bodies that little can startle him. He learns to divide his effort into separate compartments, so that while attending to one patient he does not think of the last or of the next. Moreover, he can leave the operating table or the bedside, switching off his attention, as it were, whenever he feels he has done all he can; and this judgment he can reach unfettered, since there are others to humanize it after he has gone.

Little of which applied to David's position in a girl's dressing room at the back of the pavilion on Sandmouth Pier. He did not know what more he could do, yet he did not feel he could say good-night and leave her. There was much he could have explained but for the language obstacle, at least an ease he could have given to the leave-taking. And while he was thus hesitating and wondering, a man arrived with an envelope which the girl opened; it contained a week's wages and notice of summary dismissal. She showed it, smiling wryly as she did so; then, with a shrug, she began to change out of her costume into ordinary clothes. She had no shyness.

"You see, I must go now. They will not have me any more."

"But *where* will you go?"

"Away from here. Somewhere. I don't know."

He could see she was anxious to leave before the second show ended, and he thought this was a good thing if she could manage to do it. He helped her to dress, therefore, and when she was ready they left together through a back door. Nobody seemed to notice them.

"The cold air will help you," David said, as they began to walk along the Pier towards the shore. He had to take her arm because she staggered a little. He noted that it was half-past nine; he had missed the last train to Calderbury. That meant staying overnight and taking the first train in the morning.

It was a clear night, full of stars; the chain of lights round the curve of the bay glittered across the intervening sea; the Pier lights at intervals threw moving shadows across her face. She could not walk without clinging to him for support, as he soon realized, especially when a cool wind rose into flurries. She was feeling now the full effects of the strain she had undergone, and in her touch was something remote and slumberous, as if half her consciousness were still far away, ready to respond only to a call that followed it as far. David kept silent for a long while, unwilling to disturb, even by expressing it, a sympathy which he felt was real between them. In a distant way he thought it strange that he should thus be pacing Sandmouth Pier at night, but he found it familiar that someone near him should be needing help, should fear a future. There was a sense in which he too had fear, though less personally; just that it often seemed to him that the injustice of the world could only lead to some vast and doomful reckoning. Even in the microcosm of Calderbury he felt this whenever he climbed rickety stairs to attend illness that fresh air or good food could have prevented. Something must happen some day to such a precarious social balance; cathedral bells would not always ring upon an acquiescent world. He never spoke of this, because it was in essence a mystic feeling, beyond any words in which he could convey it to anyone he had ever met. Yet with this girl he had a curious awareness that communication was possible, that the very urgency of the moment formed a link between her own hot despair and his own cool foreboding. He began to talk in a mixture of English and German. "You're not really tired of life. You're tired of pain and

63

loneliness and hopelessness. You don't really
want to die. The time to die is when you have
something to die for — the time to be tired
of life is when life is tired of you. . . ." And
so he talked, stumbling over the words, yet with
a deeper sureness that was like the breaking in
of a new instrument by a virtuoso. She clung
to him then with far more than her uninjured
arm, till at last a physical drowsiness conquered
and he knew that she was almost asleep as she
walked.

They left the Pier and threaded through the
crowds on the still frequented Promenade. He
led her to her lodgings, an apartment house
dingy even for a back street in a seaside town.
He imagined that would be the end of their
meeting, but at the house there was a surprise.
By some lightning spread of gossip, the landlady had learned of happenings at the Pier
Pavilion, with the result that she stood truculently in the front hall, hips firm and lips
tightened. "I'll have no sooicides in my
house!" came her immediate greeting, as Da-

vid helped the girl up the flight of steps to the
porch. "No turning the gas on here and blow-
ing us all up while we're in our beds! Here's
your bag — you can take it and go! And if
that's your gentleman friend I hope he knows
all about you!"

David didn't know what to do, and he was
a little upset, as he always was by scenes outside the realm of pathology. He could pacify
a frenzy within the walls of Midchester County
Asylum, but he shrank from the less tolerable
madness of those whom the world called sane.
He could think of nothing but to take the girl
away immediately, which meant to walk to the
cab stand at the corner and drive somewhere;
but of course the cabman wanted an address,
and the only one that occurred to him on the
spur of the moment was the Victoria Hotel,
where he intended to stay himself, and where
he had occasionally stayed before. So they
drove there, the girl by this time so desperately
tired that she could hardly stand up in the hotel
lobby. The clerk, recognizing David but not

65

quite sure of his name, appraised his companion curiously, wondering if she had drunk too much and if she were his wife. It was all rather odd, but none of his business; but he thought it odder still when, on being presented with the register for signature, David had to question the girl before he wrote her name. Then he wrote "Leni Krafft." He asked for two single rooms, and the clerk allotted them on the same floor. Then the doctor asked for a trunk call to Calderbury and the clerk overheard him explaining why he could n't return home that night. But (or so at any rate he said afterwards) the clerk suspected that the doctor might not be giving the right explanation.

David did not sleep well. He was puzzled and a little perturbed. He knew that in the morning he could not simply pay the two bills together, say good-bye, and never see the girl again. There comes a degree of contact where one cannot, without injury, untwist the fateful into the casual. He knew she had hardly any money. He knew she had no friends. He knew she had no job, and could not get one till her wrist had mended, and that she spoke only a few words of English. He knew her state of mind, and what it had so recently led her to attempt. He alone knew all these things about her. And he knew other things from experience, for there were folks in Calderbury, happy enough now, who at one time would have put an end to themselves but for his patient soothing of ruffled minds. It was n't that he ever argued much or was noisily cheerful; it was something that came to him instinctively out of his own feeling for the terror and beauty of life, something harmonious where all else made discord. And he had also the professional interest that every doctor takes in his patient, a desire to finish a job and pass on to another job. It was hard to know what to do in a case like this, but he well knew that to do nothing at all would be impossible for him.

In the morning they breakfasted together in

a room that faced blue seas and a sunny sky. She looked much better, having slept off most of the ill-effects of the night before; but there was still in her face the set of some profoundly tragic experience. He talked during the meal as if no problems had to be encountered, but afterwards he told her that he would lend her money which she could repay when she got another theatre job. "Sandmouth's a good place to recuperate for a few weeks — by that time your wrist ought to be better. Find some quiet lodgings where you can take things easily, then next Friday I'll call and see how you're getting on. I come here, as I told you, every Friday."

"You are so kind. . . . If everyone were as kind as you . . ."

Something in the little crushed smile she gave him as she said this made him reply: "I believe you're still worrying. Tell me what it is. Perhaps I can help you."

"No . . . no more. . . ."

"All right. I'll see you again next Friday."

68

"You are so kind," she repeated, evading the question he had hinted. But he was not really very curious.

After breakfast they found a comfortable boarding house, the sort that announced itself as a private hotel, in a street leading off the Promenade. She left her bag there and paid a week's rent in advance, for which she had money enough of her own. Then they shook hands, and she gave him the little crushed smile again, and he went off to the station to catch the morning train. He was in Calderbury by noon. It irked him to cram all his visits into half a day, but he felt some compensating satisfaction in having done one of those things he ought to have done; even more, he felt he could now put the matter completely out of his mind for a week.

CHAPTER III

THE little doctor was modest, if one had
to think of a single adjective for him;
but his modesty was more accurately a lack of
worldly ambition combined with a dislike of
comparing himself with other people. It never
occurred to him that he was a better doctor
than his colleagues (though he was), and if
anyone had suggested that this made him too
good for Calderbury, he would have replied
that nothing was too good for Calderbury. He
cared little about money or position and had
long ceased to regret the brilliant career that
had once been forecast for him and was now
out of reach. Indeed to every might-have-been
he offered the crowning indignity of forgetful-

70

ness, save when some specific reminder nudged
him.

Such a reminder was the German primer
which he took down from a dusty shelf on the
Thursday after meeting Leni in Sandmouth.
Since he had to see her the next day he thought
he might as well look over a few words. The
book brought memories of student days in London, when he had walked the wards at St.
Thomas's Hospital and lodged near by in Bat-
tersea. He had studied German then with
some idea of having a year's specializing in
Vienna, but the plan was abandoned when his
father died and left far less money than had
been expected. Feeling that he must begin
to earn something to support his mother, he
had then used up a small inheritance to buy a
general practice in a Manchester suburb, where
for several years he was both overworked and
under-rewarded. He fell ill, debts accumu-
lated, his mother died, and eventually there
was nothing left but to sell out at a loss and take
a long holiday. After this he bought the

Calderbury practice, then an inferior one, and settled down in the more congenial atmosphere of a small cathedral market town. But he still could not convert his skill and effort into anything that would pay rates and bills. He was one of those men who have no knack of extracting financial profit, and very soon he might have become that pathetic thing, a bankrupt doctor, had not Jessica taken his affairs in hand.

Jessica was a year or two older than he. Even in those days she had had a tough, leathery skin (the result of much gardening) and a rigid eye (the result of much chairmanship of small meetings). Indefatigable at the tea urn, both in drawing-rooms and in church halls, she might have made an admirable colonial bishop's wife — and, indeed, *would* have if a certain young vicar, since raised to the episcopacy, had not preferred someone far less suitable. After that she had taken pains to marry the little doctor.

And he, worried by debts (not really worried, but just bothered, for botheration was as much as anything connected with money could ever cause him), allowed himself for a short time the necessary illusion that passive willingness was really active desire.

It had been, by outward signs, a successful marriage. Jessica had reorganized all of David's life that was reorganizable; the house at the corner of Shawgate was bought with her money; and though David jibbed at complete supervision of his business affairs, her secret interferences were more frequent and more considerable than he ever suspected. She turned a loss into a profit and David gave her all the credit for doing it without any profound conviction that it was worth doing.

Friday morning came — only a few hours after he had closed the German primer at his bedside. The day promised to be fine, and as the train left Calderbury the twin towers of the Cathedral rose above a film of mist that covered the town. They looked spectral, sailing through the sky when a curve of the line kept them long in view. Presently the line crossed the water meadows to the bridge over the river, then entered a cutting. It was all such a simple thing, to travel these few miles, yet that morning it seemed to David inexpressibly strange and lovely. He opened his paper and began to read, but as soon as the train emerged from the cutting his eyes wandered again, over fields where cattle stood and where the steam from the engine, rolling in little clouds, caused them hardly to stir. Serene and secure, this world, poised on an edge it could not glimpse. The train wheels caught a rhythm which, for some reason, translated into German words, words that he must have read in the textbook the night before: —

> *Noch erkannt und sehr gering*
> *Unser Herr auf der Erde ging. . . .*

Lissington . . . Stamford Magna . . . Pumphrey . . . Marsland Junction. One changed there, and, with nothing else to do for ten minutes, one often watched the tank engine shunting round to the other end of the train, ready for the return journey to Calderbury. Then the second train came in, for Creston and Sandmouth only. The little doctor found a compartment, saw someone he knew slightly, nodded, and settled down with his paper again. For half a mile the express went back along the same line, then at the junction swerved aside to show the single track to Calderbury wandering away into a green distance. And somehow, vagrantly, the thought came to David that Calderbury was lost and that the line was trying to find it.

At Sandmouth he walked immediately to the Promenade, turning into the side street where the clifflike boarding houses soared from area basement to attic, bourgeois castles, flaunting their cruets on bay-window dining tables with an air of buxom integrity. How little it mattered where anything happened compared with what did happen; and this sense of fatefulness came to him as he climbed the flight of steps

75

that led to one of the closed front doors. He
was really rather nervous about this visit, and
with some idea of getting it over he took it
first on his list.

The landlady showed him to a room on the
first floor overlooking the street. He had not,
a week earlier, disclosed his own profession, lest
admission might be refused to a sick person;
and now he thought it simpler to keep up the
assumption of some private friendship with the
girl. He was startled a little, though he made
no comment, when the woman said: "I don't
think your young lady's very well. Maybe
it's her arm. I'd take her to see a doctor if I
were you."

A moment later he was investigating. The
girl seemed less agitated in mind — that was
something; she greeted him cheerfully. But
her wrist was still inflamed and obviously painful — which was not surprising, after her previous neglect of it. He told her frankly that
it was her own fault for not obeying the instructions he had given her at Calderbury; how

76

could she possibly have danced with broken bones chafing each other at every sudden movement? And now, as a result, the mending would be more difficult; there might even be complications; at any rate, she would have to carry her arm in a sling for weeks.

She nodded when he had finished, accepting both the situation and the blame for it. That made him smile and ask, more gently: "Do you like it here?"

She nodded and smiled back.

Yes, she was more cheerful; that was a great deal — more important, really, than her wrist.

"I think you'd better stay another week — since it seems to be doing you good. You're not lonely?"

"No."

"Made any friends?"

"The landlady's little boy. I take him for walks sometimes."

"Good. Can you understand anything he says?"

"He does n't talk a great deal. And I 'm learning English lessons from a book. I never had time before."

Up to then he had talked in German; now he said, in English: "I shall have to brush up my German, too, then we 'll be quits. Do you really like children?"

"Yes, indeed."

He had a sudden idea.

"I 've got a little boy, you know. He 's nine. It would be a change for him to come to Sandmouth, but I 've never known quite what to do with him while I make my round of visits. I wonder if . . . if I were to bring him next week . . . I could leave him in your charge for a few hours?"

"Yes, please."

"But I 'm afraid he 's not quite an ordinary little boy."

"No?"

"He 's rather nervous and excitable — and sometimes difficult — do you know what I mean?"

"I don't mind.   Please bring him."

It was just an idea, and one which, had he thought twice, he might never have put forward; for it was always possible that Jessica would object, and he disliked arguing with her. Jessica, however, was glad enough to have Gerald out of the house for a day, and quite indifferent when David explained that he had a patient at Sandmouth who had promised to act as nursemaid while he made his calls.

The arrangement, therefore, stood; but it entailed a good deal of trouble which Jessica herself would scarcely have thought worth while. David did not mind. He was careful to wait at the very front end of the stations at both Calderbury and Marsland Junction, so that the train did not rush by as it entered the station; that always terrified Gerald, and David understood as if it were the most natural thing in the world; which, indeed, he knew it was, in Gerald's world.   And then there were the actual hours of travel, during which the boy was apt to get tired and fidgety, so that he sometimes made himself a nuisance to others in the compartment.

Nevertheless, they reached Sandmouth without trouble and called immediately at the boarding house. David was a little apprehensive, because Gerald was apt to take sudden dislikes to strangers; but the first encounter seemed to him to pass well enough, and he left on a tiptoe of hopefulness that did not quite amount to confidence. When he called back later in the afternoon he found the two of them eating pink ice cream out of huge cones. "Ice cream is a thing you should *never* have unless you know where it comes from!" Jessica would have exclaimed, indignantly; but David, neither knowing nor caring where it came from, merely smiled: for the boy at that moment looked just like any other boy. It had been a dream that that should begin to happen some day.

"How did you manage?" he asked later.

"All right."

"He 's really been *good*?"

80

"Yes."

"He can't help it, you know, even when he is n't. Was n't he frightened at all — by anything?"

"He did n't like the big waves when we walked along the beach, but I made him laugh."

"You did?"

"I said things in German. I said, *'Hurtig mit Donnergepolter entrollte der tückische Marmor'* — and he began to laugh and then made me say it over and over again."

David smiled eagerly. "You know, that's just the way *I* do it too — anything to make him laugh, anything I can think of, when he gets into one of those panics. I believe that's the only way to tackle them until he can tackle them himself."

"Is it true that when he was younger he was run over by a train?"

"Good God, no! Did he say that? Oh, he's an awful little story-teller — you must n't believe everything he says. He just *imagines*

81

things, you know, and everything he imagines
is more the truth to him than what really happens. That's why he has these panics —
through imagining things. He does n't really
tell *lies*."

"I know."

"If you do know, you belong to a very small
minority, I can tell you. And I think he must
feel you do — that's why you get on so well
with him."

He had been talking English and she German most of the time. They could n't either
of them be sure that the other grasped an exact
meaning; but David did n't care. He had
never found it possible to put everything he
meant into speech; indeed, he had sometimes
felt that words offered a merely surface exactness that was both an illusion and a danger.
That was why he avoided scientific jargon, preferring to write on medical certificates "bad
cold," because he knew well enough that a bad
cold might mean anything, and that a bad cold
was in this respect rather like life. And so,

listening to Leni's German, which she no longer tried to simplify for him, he caught the mood rather than the detail, and felt no more eager to dispel an occasional word obscurity than Whistler must have wanted the mists to disappear before he would paint a sunset.

The following Friday he took Gerald to Sandmouth again. The repeated experiment was almost too successful, for the boy enjoyed himself so much that when the time came to return to Calderbury he burst into tears and refused to be comforted. That, clearly, was as big a danger as anything else; and David, promising that he should see Leni again, was privately aware that it had better not happen. It would be disastrous if Gerald should develop some deep attachment that could not continue; and how could it, since the girl would soon recover and be at work again? At least he assumed so, and she assumed so too; for her money was coming to an end, and even if she could not dance again for some time (as she certainly could not), there might be some other

temporary job to tide over the interval; they
had talked over that possibility together, and
he had been quite optimistic about her getting
a commercial post requiring knowledge of German.

They walked to the railway station, the three
of them, with these thoughts and possibilities
somewhat strangled by the need for pacifying
Gerald. He made a scene on the platform,
clinging to Leni's hand and refusing to budge.
"Good-bye," said David, harassed by all this,
as he leaned out of the window when the
struggle was over. "Good-bye — and good
luck about the job. . . ." Something in her
eyes made him add, as the guard began whistling: "By the way, if it does n't come off — the
job, I mean . . . " Then the train began to
move. "Well, write and let me know," he
added, lamely.

She did n't have to write and let him know.
Jessica wrote. Jessica, in fact, handled the situation as she always handled situations —
masterfully, with a fine eye for essentials

and a bold seizure of opportunities. She was a shrewd woman, and after Gerald's successive Fridays at Sandmouth and his delighted chatter about them, it did not take her long to realize that whatever had happened there had been fortunate. In her remarkably efficient way she wished well to the boy, though the well-wishing hardly lessened her impatience of his tantrums. If someone else had both the knack and the inclination to deal with them, then by all means let it happen. "Who *is* this woman who looks after Gerald when you're in Sandmouth?" she asked David.

David had acquired a habit of reticence about his patients' private affairs, added to which there was the vagueness that existed in his own mind when he asked himself who Leni was. Come to think about it, he simply didn't know.

"She's just a patient of mine — she broke her wrist."

"Is she a *lady?*"

David wondered, not so much whether she was or not, as whether Jessica would think her

85

one or not. At length he said: "Oh yes, I should say she is."

"Living by herself?"

"Yes."

"What sort of family?"

"She has n't any."

"Of course not, silly, if she lives by herself. I meant what kind of family does she come from?"

"I don't know — I really don't know much about her affairs."

"Is she well off?"

"Oh no, on the contrary — in fact — "

"In fact, you 've already decided not to send her a bill — I thought as much!"

"No, no — I was going to say that she 's quite poorly off — at the moment she 's trying to find work."

"She wants a job, then? I suppose she 's presentable in appearance?"

"Presentable?"

"Oh, you would n't notice, would you? You never do notice the most obvious things about

86

people.   What I 'm really wondering is if she 'd come here to help with Gerald."

"You mean to *live* here?"

"Why not, if she wants something to do?"

"Well . . ."

"You don't think she 'd come?"

"I don't know. . . .   I had n't ever thought about it."

"My dear David, you never think of anything.   Give me her address and I 'll write to her."

"The address . . . ah, let me see now — I think I can remember it — it 's the Salway Private Hotel, Beach Street."

"Her name first, stupid — I can't write without knowing that, can I?"

"Krafft — Leni Krafft."

"Goodness — it sounds foreign."

"Oh yes, I forgot to tell you — she *is* foreign — and she does n't speak much English."

"Oh, really now?   She 's not a Hottentot, by any chance, or a wild woman from Borneo? You 're always so vague about these things."

"She's German."

"Well, that's all right. At any rate it might have been worse. The Murdochs always had German governesses. What made her leave Germany?"

"I don't know."

"Well, I shall write to her, anyhow. I suppose she can understand a letter written in plain English?"

"Oh yes."

So Leni got a letter written in plain English. It offered her the job of looking after Gerald at a salary of sixty pounds a year if she proved satisfactory after a trial.

Leni came to Calderbury in March. "You'd better meet the train," said Jessica, "since you're the one who knows her"; and David said all right, he would if he got through his visits in time; otherwise Susan would have to do the recognizing as best she could. But it happened that he did finish in time, though it was dusk when he reached the station. The station-master nodded as he climbed to the platform.

"Evening, doctor. Off on your travels?"

"No. I'm just meeting somebody."

"Train's late to-night. Only just left the junction. Twenty minutes yet if you've anything else to do."

"No, thanks, I don't think I have. I'll just walk up and down."

"Well, it's good exercise, they say."

A laugh — silence — his own footsteps thudding softly on the wooden planks — chimes from the Cathedral — a quarter to five. And as he walked he began to think, really for the first time in his life, about Leni. She was coming to Calderbury. She was coming to live in his house. It was odd the way these things happened.

He watched the darkness fill the sky and absorb the lights of Calderbury into a faint glow over the roof tops. He heard five chimes from the Cathedral, the last stroke blown a little sad by a wind that suddenly veered. Then, with a whang of wire and a small answering clatter, the signal fell. The train emerged from the

89

cutting across the river, clanked over the iron bridge, and came streaking through the water meadows like a familiar friendly ghost. Whereat Calderbury's one porter held himself ready for the improbable event of anyone requiring his services. "G'd evening, doctor."

They talked for a moment about the porter's little girl, who had been ill and was now recovering.

The train was in.

"Shall I take 'is luggage, sir?"

"Whose luggage?"

"Your friend's. Thought you was meeting a friend."

"Oh yes . . . but . . . it's a lady. I don't know whether she 'll have any luggage. Well, maybe she will. . . . Yes, take it down!"

She was already stepping out of the train, carrying a suitcase and a wicker basket.

"Leni!"

"Oh, du kleine doktor!"

They did n't know what else to say to each other at first. There was the business of hand-ing over the luggage, surrendering her ticket, passing the barrier with the small crowd from the train. People who knew David kept up a chorus of good-evenings. On the way down the steps to the street level he said: "Gerald's looking forward to your arrival."

Leni exclaimed in German: "I could n't believe I was really coming!"

"It was Jessie's idea — I don't know why I never thought of it myself."

The porter, walking ahead, pricked up his ears. Afterwards he reported: "They did n't talk much, but when the doctor said something she answered in some foreign lingo and 'e seemed to understand it all right from the way he smiled back at 'er. . . ."

CHAPTER IV

LENI settled down at the house in Shawgate
and Gerald was happy. It was miracu-
lous, the success she had in calming the boy's
nervousness and brightening his moods whenever they darkened; she could do it as well as
David, and, of course, the trouble had always
been that David had so little time for doing
it. Now, instead of Jessica's rigid discipline
of scoldings and repetitions, Leni imposed her
more elastic sway; and Jessica, freed from an
irksome duty, seemed satisfied. David was
satisfied too. After the first surprise of Leni's
presence he regarded it with sudden simplicity.
It was his mission far more to mend what was
wrong than to question what was right, and

her position in his household soon appeared to him as unarguably right as a flower or the morning mail delivery. For just as he had a childlike inquisitiveness on the surface, so he was apt to seem incurious when he knew people better, not from any lack of interest, but because of his complete acceptance of them as they were. And if someone had suggested that there was anything odd in a German ex-stage dancer becoming his son's governess, he would first of all have had to recollect that she *was* a German ex-stage dancer, and then have answered, with complete sincerity, that it was no odder than anything else. He wasn't bothered, for instance, by any mystery there might be about her name and past; it did not seem to matter to him since he called her Leni and liked her. He called everyone by their first names.

Gradually her wrist became stronger and one afternoon, when Jessica was out, David heard her playing the piano. It was more from the surgical than the musical angle that he viewed this experiment; he wished to see how far the fracture had impaired her finger movements. To his considerable surprise she began to play rather well, and things he had never heard before; they were n't his kind of music, anyway. Then he put in front of her a Mozart Sonata, thinking he might give himself the pleasure of hearing it; but she shook her head. "I can't read it," she told him.

"What? You can't read music?"

"Only very slowly."

"Then how do you learn all these things?"

"Mostly from ear."

"You mean you 've never been *taught* music?"

She shook her head a third time.

"Well, it 's very remarkable. You certainly ought to have training."

"May I practise while I am here?"

"Why, certainly. You 'll find a lot of classical stuff in the cabinet — my own tastes."

"You play the piano?"

"The violin — but not much. What time does a doctor have?"

And he went away to his daily duties, vaguely wondering whether he should introduce her to Jaggers, the Cathedral organist, or to Yule, the Cathedral choirmaster, and let them share his discovery. Perhaps they might even give her lessons. And perhaps at the musical party he usually gave once a year he might ask her to play something. That would n't be a bad idea at all.

After that, and mostly during the afternoons when Jessica was out, Leni played the piano in the drawing-room. He did n't realize what she was doing until one day, by accident, he came in and heard her playing the piano part of the Kreutzer Sonata. He stood outside the drawing-room door and listened till she had finished. Then he entered.

"But you learned that from music?"

"It was very slow and difficult for me to pick out the notes, but when I had done that, then

I knew it from memory.   I 've been practising a lot lately."

"Fine.   But I still think you ought to have some proper training."

Smilingly he walked away, again registering an intention of talking to Jaggers or Yule about her.   But at the back of his mind in such a matter there was always the thought of Jessica; she might not approve — one could never prophesy her attitude.   After fifteen years of married life he had acquired an intense reluctance to make decisions of any kind outside his own immediate professional territory; only by such reluctance was he insulated against the kind of conflict in which, because it would so intensely bore him, he could not fight to any advantage.

So he did not actually mention Leni to Jaggers or Yule or, indeed, to anyone; but he went on thinking he ought to do, and *must* do, and perhaps would do so, one of those days.

But one of those days, a July day, David returned to Calderbury after his weekly visit to

Sandmouth.   There had been showers during the afternoon, but by evening the sky had totally cleared, and as he walked from the railway station the towers of the Cathedral seemed to exude a memory of both sunshine and rain. It was very beautiful at such a time, especially the view over the town, the mist rising above roofs, a hint of human cosiness in all that huddle of buildings.   As David crossed the Close a lamplighter stopped near by, his face upturned to the glow he made.

"Good night, doctor."

"Good night, Ben."

Suddenly, walking on towards Shawgate, he met Leni.   "Why —" he began, as if he had not seen her for years.   She stopped, smiling but silent.   "Taking a walk?" he said.

"Just for a while."

There came into the air a murmur that might have been anything or nothing till one realized what it was.

"Choir practice," she said, answering his thought.   "I have heard it before."

"Do you often take a turn round here, then?"

"Take a turn? What is that?"

He put it into German for her, and then a curious line of her mouth, lit by the merging of twilight and lamplight, gave him an impression of mishap that made him add: "Is anything the matter?"

She answered, in German also: "Mrs. Newcome has told me I must go."

"*What?*"

"Yes."

"Must *go?* But where?"

"Away."

"But why — why on earth — should she say that?"

"She said she can't afford to have me."

"But that's absurd. We can afford it perfectly well."

"She said not."

A silence fell on them both, and into it, making an interruption, came the voice of a passer-by: "G'night, doctor."

"Good night," answered David, not knowing, never knowing indeed, who the other was. Then he turned to Leni. "I really don't understand it. I must see what Jessica has to say."

Without the suggestion made or accepted they walked together down Shawgate, saying little else. Leni walked so quietly at his side, asking no questions that he could not answer, not bothering him, not making any fuss. Absurd to say one could n't afford such rare and priceless negations. Lamplight caught her face as she glanced sideways to cross streets, and he noticed, till it began to preoccupy him, the look of calmness that matched perfectly with her silence. Even her despair had held that same calmness. And suddenly he remembered the dressing room where she had tried to end her life, the Pier where they had walked that night, the already mounting total of their experience. Absurd that now, after so much, she should go. He must talk to Jessica as soon as he had the chance, though he realized, even in making that decision, how little he cared to ask Jessica anything. It was n't that he was really afraid of her, or that there was truth in Calderbury's popular notion that she ruled him with a rod of iron. He was n't; she could n't. It was rather that his own will to do what he liked in his own house had been worn into a shrug of the shoulders that yielded, by nonchalance, all that could never have been claimed by force. Furthermore, Jessica was so efficient that it was easy to let her encroach to the very rampart of self-preservation; and that rampart, for David, was the door of the surgery.

Jessica was writing invitations when he found her later in the drawing-room. The engraved cards, filled in with handwritten names, lay spread out on the writing desk beside her — "Dr. and Mrs. Newcome request the pleasure of . . ."

"Jessie," he began, breathlessly and without preamble. "What 's all this about getting rid of Leni?"

Jessica faced him with her thin, well-chiseled

face, faced him also with her no-nonsense personality at full strength.

"Yes, it 's quite true.   I told her she could n't
stay."

"But why?"

"I had my reasons, I assure you."

"But it 's absurd to say we can't afford her
wage! She 's well worth it — Gerald likes
her enormously — "

"That was only the reason I gave *her*. It
was n't the *real* reason."

"What was that?"

"Do you really need me to tell you?"   Her
voice sharpened to the pitch in which, at meetings of this or that, she usually called some
errant speaker to order.   "Has it ever occurred
to you that people are n't always what they
seem?   I was far too trusting to take that girl
without the usual inquiries, but I was relying
— foolishly, no doubt — on your own as-
surance.   I might have guessed how little you
really knew of her.   And I must say, too, that
I did n't *take* to her, even from the first."

Jessica was like that. She had a way of finding that she did n't like people and then of saying that she never had liked them — thus imputing clairvoyance to herself and vaguely sinister attributes to her victims.

"I don't quite know, Jessie, what you 're driving at."

"Oh, you don't? I 'm glad you admit it. You don't know, I suppose, that this girl was on the stage a few months back, doing a dance turn in fifth-rate shows? And you don't know that she was dismissed because she tried to commit suicide!"

"Oh yes," said David, simply, "I knew all that."

Quite unconscious of having spoiled Jessica's moment, his only thought was a reassuring one — that if *that* was all the trouble, what could the fuss be about?

Jessica's voice keyed up another half-tone. "So you *knew*? And you never told me?"

"I never like to gossip about a patient's private affairs."

102

"How very considerate to your patients! But hardly to your family! Did you *really* think a suicidal stage dancer — and a foreigner, at that — was the kind of person to have in a respectable household and look after a nervous child?"

David blinked a little, thinking of Leni and of how silly it was to try to pin down the truth about people in words, because the words could all be true and yet have no truth in them. "She's all right, my dear," he said quietly.

"You call her all right? . . . I've no patience with you, David. Apart from the risk of heaven knows what, don't you think there's enough scandal all over the town now that this story's got about? Do you know she once appeared on the stage at the theatre here?"

"Yes, that was where she broke her wrist last December. I attended her."

"Well, *really!* You knew all that and did n't say a thing!"

103

David was silent, and Jessica too. After a long pause she commented: "A queer business. Right from the first moment I was certain there was something queer about it."

" But there is n't."

"There must be, if she 's the sort that tries to commit suicide."

"Oh, no, Jessie. It is n't queer people who do that — it 's people just like everyone else — — like you or me — if ever we were driven to it."

"Well, I don't want to argue. She 's got to go, that 's all."

"But Gerald — "

"He must learn to manage without her. I 'm sure she 's doing him no real good."

Then David, planting himself firmly on a small fragment of endangered territory, took a stand which was all the more obstinate for being minute. He was not really a good fighter. He hated squabbles and it was never easy for him to grasp such issues as could be involved in them. "She can't go before the end of the month," he said, as if pronouncing a moral dictum or an immutable law.

"She can if I pay her."

"It is n't a matter of paying. You can't act suddenly like this and make her find new work and new lodgings at a moment's notice."

"I don't see that her future plans have anything to do with us."

"Maybe not, but I think we ought to treat her as a human being. We can't just give her a few shillings and put her out in the street."

"You say we can't?"

"I say we must n't."

"Very well, if that's your attitude she shall stay till her month is finished — which means another fortnight of her company. But don't expect me to leave Gerald with her. *You* can look after the girl's interests; *I* prefer to look after my own child's. . . . And now tell me about these invitations to the musical party — do you want the Cowens to come this year or not?"

David shook his head bewilderedly and walked to the door. When he got there he said "Ask them if you like," and passed into the corridor. He moved absently for a few paces, then his feet led him down the three familiar steps and through the green-baize-covered double doors into the surgery. There, entrenched in his own domain, he felt a little but not greatly eased. Of course it was quite true that in a cathedral town there was a lot of gossip, and Jessica, nearer to it in her daily contacts, was probably surer in reckoning its importance. And also, of course, so long as Leni could get another job as good or better, it did n't really matter to her. He would write her a testimonial if she was n't fit for a theatre job, and perhaps, with her knowledge of German, she might find work as a teacher or in some firm. And though he would personally miss her, and he knew Gerald would too, her absence could only put back everything as it had been before, even for the boy. He smoked for a while and tried in vain to put the whole confusing issue out of his mind; till at last, far after midnight, his thoughts grew weary, pacifying him into a sense of communion with all other souls awake at that hour, with every striving puzzling soul beneath the roofs of Calderbury.

When he saw Leni in the morning as he left for his round of visits he behaved as if nothing particular had happened. He was aware of a directly personal relationship between them, aware of it as never before; it touched something in him which was as solitary as itself. When he returned about noon Leni told him that Jessica had taken Gerald away and that the boy had made a scene.

"When he said good-bye to you?"

"He was n't allowed to say good-bye to me."

"Do you know where Jessie took him?"

"To Mr. Simpson."

"Oh yes, my wife's brother. He's Vicar of St. Peter's. Nice fellow — he's looked after Gerald before."

"Do you think he 'll be happy?"

"Gerald? I don't know." He leaned against the edge of the desk and began tapping it with his fingernail. "I 'm sorry it 's all happened like this. I really am. But what can I do about it? I 'm not one of those people who like to make trouble. Sometimes — sometimes I wish I were."

"Don't worry," she said. He knew her sympathy, yet felt it as a spell he must break at all costs.

"Has Jessie come back?" he asked.

"No, not yet. She said she 'd be out for lunch."

"Then . . . I won't have any lunch. Just a cup of coffee and a sandwich here. Will you tell Susan?"

"I told Susan. I knew you always had that when Mrs. Newcome 's away."

"See that you get something yourself."

" I 'm not hungry either."

Over the murmur of Calderbury activities there came the twang of the street piano that

108

always moved along Shawgate on Thursday market days, pushed by an old wooden-legged character named Joe Moore. Presently Susan entered with a plate of sandwiches and coffee. "You must have some," David said to Leni, thinking she might as well eat and drink in the surgery as anywhere else. He smiled and then had to add: "I talked to Jessie, by the way, last night — and I'm sorry — personally I'm very sorry indeed — "

"You mean I have to go?"

"Not for a fortnight."

"But now that Gerald's gone — "

"I know, but I made Jessie agree to the fortnight."

The fortnight was offered between them as a symbol of the extent to which he had argued with Jessica and opposed her; as a gesture indicating action which, had he been inclined for any, he would have taken; as, finally, a gift which could not be refused.

"Because, you see, during that fortnight we'll have time to find you another job."

She nodded.

"Or else, if we can't, then I'll pay your fare back to Germany."

Something in her change of expression served then as a reminder, so that he went on, hastily: "Oh, but I forgot — you said you did n't want to go back, did n't you?"

"I can't go back."

He accepted the statement as if it were only just beginning to occur to him how little he knew about her, as well as how remarkably little he had ever bothered to know.

". . . Because I ran away," she added suddenly.

"From home?"

"No — from school. . . . It was very strict and I hated it. The Russian frontier was quite close, so I ran away one night and went to St. Petersburg, to the dance school there, but the police found out about me, so I had to run away again. I hid myself on a ship in the docks and came to London. So you see I must stay in England now — I cannot go back to

Germany. They would arrest me there —
because of the forgery."

"Forgery? Why, what was that?"

"On the passport when I went to Russia.
You have to have a passport. I altered all the
writing on the certificate — about my name
and age. I just made up a name."

He began to smile. "But it was n't done
with any criminal intent. I don't suppose
you'd find the authorities very hard on you.
They would n't send you to prison."

"Not to the prison, maybe, but back to the
school."

He laughed. "Oh really, no — they could n't
do that. At your age you've a perfect
right — "

"No, no, that's just it — because on the
passport I said I was twenty-five."

"And are n't you?"

"I'm nineteen."

David looked at her. He had never really
wondered about her age, but now he realized
that he was astonished. Nineteen! It did n't,

of course, make any difference to the way he would treat her. He never condescended to youth, never behaved as if seniority gave him superiority. There was a sense in which he treated grown-ups as if they were children; but in the same sense he also treated children as if they were grown-ups. And there was this same childlike gravity in the readiness with which he believed people, because he knew he knew so little about the nature of truth, except that it could be very strange indeed.

"You won't tell anyone, will you? Not even the police — if they come to ask about me?"

He touched her reddish hair, thinking it now a child's. "I would n't worry at all if I were you."

"No, I do not worry now. Because you do not worry, either. You never ask me about anything and that was why I have told you everything."

In the lives of most Calderbury citizens there was little that one might count the days to,

either in fear or in anticipation. Months flowed
by in a stream of busy uneventfulness, varied
by occasions that arrived almost before one
realized they were due: Christmas, Easter,
Whitsun, the summer holidays; market day,
Sunday, the monthly diocesan gazette, quar-
terly payments, the annual fair. From the
bishop's to the butcher's, Calderbury lives were
signposted thus, and years drove past without a gear change. Only the schoolboy
crossing off dates to the end of term, or the
old-age pensioner in fear of next winter's
chills, could taste the cruel beauty that time
offers to those who are bound to count its
fragments.

Something of that cruel beauty entered the
doctor's house in Shawgate, touching him every
morning as he rose and every evening when he
had said good-night to his last surgery caller
and there was nothing left but to smoke and
go to bed. He preferred those final moments
of the day alone, for he was, beyond outward
fellowship and impersonal altruism, a solitary,

aware of communion with life itself rather than with individual lives.

But now, meeting Leni from time to time during the diminishing fortnight, a little of that calmness was dislodged. He saw her sometimes during the afternoons, when she played the piano in the drawing-room; once he got out his violin and began a sonata with her, but in the middle of it he heard Jessica entering the house and talking to Susan, so he made an excuse to discontinue the performance. He knew Jessica disliked music, and he had never found it possible to enjoy playing when she was at home. He said, putting his violin back in the case: "We must finish that some-time. And I must see about lessons for you — you really ought to have them, you know." He kept saying that, but he never did anything about it.

He knew, though she did not tell him, how little she wished to leave, yet how hard it was to stay, even those few more days. For Jessica, by pricks of word and action, was always indicating the obvious — that there was nothing to stay for, no work to do, no reason why she should not take her money and quit. The days passed slowly, braked by a curious brooding uncomfortableness; David, busy with his work, saw neither Jessica nor Leni for any length of time; yet whenever he entered the house he felt their presence in distant separate rooms. Perhaps it had been a mistake to insist on that fortnight; he thought so when, taking meals with Jessica, he measured her cold, controlled civility against the thoughts that might lie behind it. But when, at other times, he met Leni in the hall, or in the corridor outside the surgery, her smile made him feel that the fortnight was beautiful, with a beauty sharpened by all that made it unwise.

He fretted, too, about Gerald and how he was faring, and once, after his day's work, the news in the evening paper gave him a vision of human mischief larger, but no more wanton, than that which had invaded his own affairs. Seeking escape from an intolerable perception, he went out, took the path by the river, and climbed the Knoll. The vast unreason of the world assailed him, as well as a sense of his own unfitness for battle; and suddenly, with rueful self-scrutiny, he saw himself as he must seem to others, perhaps even to Leni — a weak-willed middle-aged husband who dared not say no to his wife. Yet it was n't really that he dared not. It was a profounder reluctance, an inertia of the spirit that fell on him whenever he faced a conflict outside the territory in which he could struggle with joy. To fight the blood flow as it streamed into the cavity of an operation, to fight the weakening of lungs and heartbeat, to fight death and the fear of death — these were his battles and he had no strength or will for others.

He walked on, as far as the little wooden hut on the hill, and during a pause to light his pipe someone (he could not see who at first) came up to him and said something.

"Leni!" he exclaimed, and then found himself speechless with surprise.

"Yes, I often come here in the evenings. Have you any news of Gerald?"

David flinched at the question. "Yes, I call and see him every day."

"How is he?"

"Not very happy, I 'm afraid."

"It is so silly that I cannot still look after him."

They walked on silently, and in a little gap of moonlight between the trees he began to study the outline of her face, the long slender nose, the forehead straight and ample. All at once he knew that he had her in memory forever, could trace that profile with closed eyes, every curve and line in precious ease to his imagination.

"What are you thinking about?"

"You and what is to happen to you."

"I shall get a job."

"Yes, and next time you ought n't to go in for these second-rate things — Pierrots at the seaside and the kind of show you were in when you first came here. I think you ought to try some really good theatre — in London."

She smiled, knowing the absurdity of it all. Their worlds were different, their ages were different, their lives and languages were different; yet all those differences became themselves absurd when measured against the flash of recognition that sprang between them at every nearness. She said, touching his arm as she walked: *"Ah . . . du kleiner Doktor . . .* I am not so good as that. . . . You have never seen me dance, have you?"

He shook his head. "What sort of dancing do you do?"

"Some day I would like to show you. But I am not very good. Maybe if I could have stayed in Petersburg and worked hard for years at the school there — "

He said, quite seriously: "Yes, I'm afraid we haven't any good dancing school in Calderbury. It's a pity your career had to be interrupted."

"But I have been so happy here," she answered.

CHAPTER V

IT had been David's habit for many years to give a party during the latter half of July, a sort of garden party with music, to which all the notables of Calderbury society were invited. If the weather was warm and fine the French windows were thrown open to the walled garden, and the guests sat about in or out of doors as they chose. No other function in Calderbury's year offered quite the same features, but it was generally considered that the doctor had established a right to be original and that his party was among the events of the social season. In truth, the originality had arisen merely from the fact that Jessica had wanted a garden party in summer while the doctor preferred a musical evening in winter, and neither wanted both. David had, indeed, a quiet liking for music that led him to join the Calderbury Philharmonic Society and play the violin in string quartets.

It was during the second week of Leni's last fortnight that the party was to take place. All day the sun had shone so warmly that one of Shawgate's pavements had been deserted and the other crowded with shade-seeking shoppers. Jessica, always insistent on getting precisely what she wanted and at the most economical price, was among them; the tradesmen respected her for the qualities that made her visits a trial. Besides, they knew the doctor's party was to be in the evening and that somebody would say, "Do tell me, Mrs. Newcome, where you got these delicious preserves?"

While she was shopping, Sam Bates, the electrician, was running a few colored lights under the cedar tree in the doctor's garden, and Johnny Johnson, the odd-job gardener, was erecting trestle tables, arranging chairs on the lawn, and generally making himself useful. The doctor was visiting; Susan was baking pies for the evening; Leni was doing simply nothing.

By special arrangement there was to be no surgery session, and David, as soon as he got home, took a tepid bath and changed into a different suit of clothes that looked exactly the same. The invitations were for eight o'clock, by which time the heat of the day had drained into walls and pavements, leaving the air cool. The sky was clear, and a half-moon rose over the cedar tree.

About fifty people gathered and grouped in the drawing-room and garden — the Dean and the Archdeacon, the Precentor, Jaggers the organist, Yule the choirmaster, various vicars of parishes, doctors, a solicitor, a retired admiral, the headmaster of the local grammar school, the editor of the *Calderbury Gazette*. But there the edge was reached of that social territory beyond which Mrs. Newcome would not venture; and it was tacitly understood that

Fred Garton, son of the town's leading grocer and invited because of his fine baritone, was not really a guest in the same sense as the others.

Greetings, gossip, a piano solo by the choir-master, who did not play very well, and for whom the doctor's piano would not have been good enough if he had; then a Grieg violin solo by the wife of the grammar-school head. In the midst of this, Susan entered with a message which made David tiptoe from the room, followed by glances of vague commisera-tion. "It's always like that for a doctor, isn't it?" people said to Jessica afterwards, and she admitted that it was. Actually she didn't feel that David's absence mattered very much, since he was no help in running any but a children's party.

He cycled to a cottage in Colohan Street, off Briargate; a workman, his wife, and six chil-dren lived there in four small rooms. One of the six lay gasping and coughing in bed. "Bronchial, doctor," the father kept saying, with the pathetic trustfulness of the man who knows a word. David soon found that it was double pneumonia. There was little chance for the boy, who was about the same age as Gerald; it was a case that should have been under skilled treatment days before. David did what he could, left instructions with the plaintively glum parents, and promised to send a nurse immediately and call again about midnight. Said the man timorously: "Will a nurse cost much, doctor?" — and David answered, as on so many other occasions, "Oh no, no, very little — I 'll arrange it." Downstairs, as the woman edged him along the narrow lobby past a perambulator, she said: "You know, we used to have Dr. Thompson, but Mrs. Nickle who 's just come to live next door put in a word for you." "God bless my soul," thought David momentarily, "she thinks she 's doing me a favor calling me in to attend a neglected pneumonia that I 'll never get paid for and that I 'll probably be blamed for not being able to save!" But he said, touched by sympathy that lay deeper: "Yes, indeed, I remember Mrs. Nickle . . ."

But back on his bicycle he forgot Mrs. Nickle and only thought of the fluid spreading and thickening in strained lungs, the word "bronchial" that had killed just as another word might have saved, the chatter of women over garden fences, recommending doctors as they might tip horses. . . . Stupid, pathetic, suffering world.

By the time he returned to the house the party had had the refreshment interval and were on with music again. He let himself in by the surgery entrance. Passing through the waiting room, he caught the sound of strings; then, as he opened the surgery door, the sound swelled into sudden harmony, and also, at the same moment, he saw Leni in the leather armchair.

She looked so still and calm, so much a part of all that he sought beyond the fret of existence, that he caught his breath at both the sight and the sound; and all at once he realized something that he had long been experiencing without notice — an unclenching of every nerve whenever he came into her presence, a secret renewal of strength to take up every stress when he was left alone.

"Was it anything serious, David?"

"Not only serious but hopeless, I'm sorry to say."

(A way they often had, and a way that no one else had ever had with him, to begin talking without preliminaries, as if speech were suddenly switched on to a conversation that had been taking place for a long time, but silently.)

"I am sorry too."

He put down his hat and bag and sat in the swivel desk chair and was soon absorbed. Something in music rarely failed to lure him with a promise. He was no facile optimist, and nothing of his secret belief could be expressed in any outward allegiance to party or creed; he had no wild faith in progress, even in his own craft. But the patience and patterning of a string quartet offered him the strongest hint of destiny in man — and destiny without deans. It was not that he was irreligious — merely that a whiff of anticlericalism flavored his musings when he had a house full of Cathedral dignitaries. He was really happier by himself in the surgery, and "by himself" did not conflict with the presence of Leni. So why join the crowd just yet?

"I ought to have been playing in that quartet," he said, when it was over. "But listen — " Fred Garton was beginning to sing. He had a good voice and a musicianly intelligence. "I don't think I ever heard that song before."

"It is a song by Schubert called 'Die Krähe.' From the *Winterreise*."

"*Krähe*? What's that?"

"I don't know what you call it. A bird — black — disastrous — I can't think of the word."

"Never mind. . . . Leni, I'm sorry you're going."

"Six . . . more . . . days. . . ."

126

"And four of them I'm away at a conference. It's too bad. I shall miss you."

"I shall miss you too. . . . Oh, that word —'Die Krähe'—I can remember now—it means a bird that Poe wrote a poem about."

"The raven?"

They looked up and saw Jessica standing outside the door, opening it slowly.

Fred Garton's song drew an encore, and it was during this that Jessica returned to the drawing-room with David. It was noticed that he looked pale and weary, from which observers were ready to deduce an arduous errand.

But Jessica gave him no peace. It was not that she was deliberately uncivil, or that any actual thing she said could have been objected to, but rather that she put him in positions where he was constantly at a disadvantage. "David, Mr. Campbell can't see his music — switch on the light over the piano, will you, please." As most of the lights had been put

127

out for the music, David had a choice of a dozen switches; and it was a little comic when he kept pressing the wrong ones. "I thought you knew," said Jessica coolly, when he had at last succeeded. And then later: "David will turn over the pages for you, Mrs. Shapkey." There was no reason at all why David should; he was n't good at reading piano music, and at nearly every turn he was so late that the pianist had to give him an agitated signal. Afterwards he apologized, but Jessica cut in with: "Don't believe him, Mrs. Shapkey — it is n't that he can't read, it 's just that he does n't pay attention." She laughed as she spoke, making it sound harmless, but the laugh itself was unyielding.

Finally she bothered him at the doorway with the hats. That was Susan's job, not David's, but of course he had to respond when she said: "David, have you seen Mr. Driveway's hat? Do look for it." He could n't refuse to join the search; on the other hand, what use was it to pick up hats at random when

Mr. Driveway was so much more likely to dis-
cover his own?

Just little things like that.

And presently the guests departed; all grew
quiet in the doctor's house. At midnight he
bicycled to the cottage where the boy lay dying
of pneumonia but still alive. David stayed
till four; then, with eyes hardly open, bicycled
back through the dawn-lit streets. He did not
go to bed, but slumped into the surgery chair
and wakened at half-past seven, made himself
a cup of tea, and cycled to the local infirmary.
It was a small institution on the edge of the
town, fairly well equipped, and efficiently man-
aged. David as a rule looked forward to his
visits there, preferring the orderliness of the
wards to the cramped sickrooms of private
houses; but that morning as he half dozed
along the roads he could only think of the
extraordinary fret and muddle that had en-
compassed him — he did not see what he could
do about it, it all seemed so preposterous. He
left the bicycle in the shed and walked in

through the main doors of the hospital so slowly and vagrantly that a couple of nurses, watching from a window, commented upon his air of preoccupation. In the anteroom where he put on his surgeon's uniform he was still oppressed with the revelation of a wantonly misbehaving world. Trevor, his young assistant, and Jones, the anæsthetist, had already arrived.

"Going to be a warm one to-day, doctor."

"Yes, indeed."

"Feeling the heat? You look tired."

"Oh, just a bit sleepy, that's all. How's the case?"

"All ready for you." And Jones added, rather nervously: "Difficult, do you think?"

Then, as at a signal, David's manner changed. No longer was he the tired man harassed by the chafings of events, but a reserve power that could be tapped immediately by anyone who craved it. Young Jones was new and not yet very expert; he had bungled once or twice before and had blamed himself into a state of nervousness. David took him by the arm, sensing and combating his anxieties. "Oh, I would n't call it difficult, Fred. Just watch the pulse and be ready for transfusions."

They passed into the theatre together, and there, even if nowhere else, the little doctor was in his kingdom.

At that time patients were usually anæsthetized on the table with all the apparatus of surgery to add panic to their trepidation. But David, always aware of fear as a poison in the blood, would never allow the more suggestive items to be exposed to that last frightened consciousness — instruments, clamps, sponges, and so on. Trays containing these were covered over till ether or nitrous oxide had begun its work; and this, among the hospital staff, was regarded as just one of the little doctor's fads. He had several others.

The patient lay outstretched, with pain-sharpened eyes swerving restlessly amidst his new environment. He was an old man, night watchman at a factory, grey-haired and thin-featured, the thinness accentuated by disease. His hands, loosely taped to the cross rests, were white and wasted, but emaciation could not hide the seams and scars of a hard-working lifetime. The hipbones, almost fleshless, lifted the covering sheet into ridges.

"Nothing to worry about, Charlie," David said, smiling as he touched the pulse for a moment. He always called his patients by their names when they were on the table, because he believed it primed a man with some personal dignity when he lay pinioned and anxious under the glare.

David nodded to Jones and the stream of stupefying gas began to pour into nostrils and lungs, while the battery of arcs, now switched full on, shone down on a shrouded human body, shrouded except for a stained rectangle of flesh that rose and sagged irregularly. The little doctor stood by, like an actor waiting for his cue; presently he uncovered a tray of instruments and arranged them, giving instructions to the nurses in a low muttering. "More clamps here, sister . . . smaller ones. . . . Too much iodine — wash a little off with alcohol. . . . Sponges . . . smaller ones . . . no, never cut a sponge . . . the man's very thin, that's a help. . . . How's he going, Jones?"

Sometimes, waiting at such moments, he felt that his words were like an incantation, and the thought came to him that if, twenty thousand years ago, human eye could have looked ahead to glimpse the supine victim, the tray of instruments, the white-gowned and masked officiants, it could only have deduced some scene of ritual torture.

Jones signaled and David began, calmly confident, at home with the familiar feel of the knife ploughing through skin and flesh, so swiftly that the first reddening crept into the slope of the cavity almost like a blush. Deeper . . . then the click of the clamps as the nurses handed them. . . . "There . . . another one . . . lay them outside the gauze . . . now a retractor. . . ." Precision hypnotized the

133

room and its occupants; the minutes passed as in a dream which only the hands of the clock could certify. "He was a fine surgeon," Trevor said, long afterwards. "You watched his hands and had an impression at first that they were behaving automatically — then you realized a perfect coördination between brain and muscle, a quiet fearless exactness that was almost boring after a time, like championship billiards.   After all, it's the mistakes that make drama — and God knows there were doctors in Calderbury who made drama enough of that kind — fellows who had the whole hospital staff in a state of nerves if they were only going to lance an abscess. . . .   But the little doctor, as we called him, made everyone as calm as himself.   And he had a curious way — a sort of mystic way, if you let yourself be fanciful about it — of looking up and blinking while his fingers told him things. He'd put his hand inside an abdomen as far as the wrist and feel around and just mutter to himself and to youngsters like me who were looking

134

on: 'No, there's no pelvic inflammation . . .
rather a small spleen . . . oh dear, that's too
bad — C.A. just here. . . .' He made us always say 'C.A.' even amongst ourselves, lest
otherwise the fatal word might slip out in front
of patients; but of course some of 'em were
cute enough to suspect what the initials meant,
and then he'd tell the most fantastic lies about
them. Often he'd make up a disease with a
flower name like Calceolaria or Caprifoliaceæ,
and when once we reminded him that the
patient might, after all, know something about
gardening, he said: 'Well, that's all right —
it's a nice association of ideas — can't do any
harm. And diseases *are* like flowers — they
seed and grow and spread. . . .' God, he had
some crazy ideas — yet there was something
great about him, too — something that made
you want to worship him at times."

And Jones, who afterward conquered his
nervousness and became an anæsthetist in a
big city hospital, commented when he was
prosperous and successful: "Yes, I used to work

under Newcome at Calderbury. He was damn
nice to me, say what you like about him. He'd
have had a career, that man, if he hadn't
stuck in Calderbury — well, maybe he
wouldn't — he wasn't the kind to use his
chances properly. Funny little chap, rather
like a wise child, but not wise enough for
municipal politics. Didn't know which side
his bread was buttered on."

"What do you mean by that?"

"Oh, well, Mrs. Newcome was all in with
the Cathedral crowd — great opening for Newcome in a place like Calderbury if he'd played
his cards properly. As it was . . . well, there
was one incident: Newcome was going round
the wards — he'd been operating — and Archdeacon Rogers was going round too, doing *his*
stuff — you remember what a pompous fellow
he was? If you knew Calderbury, I'm sure
you *do* remember. Anyhow, in the corridor
after the grand tour he kept Newcome and me
talking, wasting our time, in point of fact, and
one of the things he said was that a surgeon

in the course of his job was bound to acquire respect for the mind of God in creating such a wonderful thing as the human body. Of course when parsons talk like that one does n't usually say anything — bad form, you know, as well as pretty useless. But Newcome answers in that mild soft-toned voice he had: 'I 've just been operating on an enlarged prostate, and, believe me, any intelligent plumber could invent a better drainage system than you and I possess, Archdeacon!' Of course old Rogers was terribly shocked — I believe that was why he used his influence to prevent Newcome being offered the medical officership."

David had begun the operation on Charlie at eight o'clock in the morning; the final stage was not complete until after ten. It had been an awkward case, largely inoperable, and complicated by a weak heart. Twice the man had almost died on the table. But at last, still breathing faintly, and with bandages like a great white bundle tied in front of him, he was wheeled away to hours of lingering uncon-

sciousness, days of pain, a few months of half-
life, pain again, and death.

David pulled off the stained gloves and
washed his hands and face in the lavatory ad-
joining the theatre. As always after an operation he felt the sudden deflation of personal
ascendancy; he had given himself, and was
now utterly spent. Rallying himself a little,
he visited a few of his patients in the wards;
then he rode away for his usual morning round
of house calls. One of them was the pneumonia he had been called to the night before;
to his surprise and gratification the boy was a
little better.

He was late home for lunch and was neither
startled nor disconcerted when Susan greeted
him with: "Mrs. Newcome would n't wait,
sir."

"Oh, I don't mind — all I want is some
coffee."

"She asked if you would go in and see her."

"Eh? Where? Why? What does she
want?"

"I don't know, sir. She's in the dining room."

"Oh, all right, I'll go."

Because he was used to obeying in these small outward things, he went. Jessica had finished lunch and was toying with biscuits and cheese.

"Really, David, I couldn't wait for you — I really do think you might try to be punctual for at least one occasion of the day — "

"It's all right. I'm glad you didn't wait."

"I suppose you've got the usual excuse of having had an exceptionally busy morning."

"Well yes, I have been rather busy."

"I'm sorry you preferred to stay in the surgery rather than join your guests last night."

He said nothing.

"Did you *invite* that girl into the surgery?"

He said nothing.

"What business had she in there?"

He said nothing.

"A good job she's leaving in a few days, anyhow."

He said nothing.

"Are you too tired to answer me?"

Suddenly his nerves chafed to a raw edge he could barely endure. He said: "Yes, I'm rather tired. I'm sorry for the boy's sake, that's all."

"What are you talking about?"

"I just don't see any point in sending her away or in sending him away."

"I don't understand you."

"I'm talking about Leni."

"Oh, you are? I understand *that,* of course. It's quite obvious why *you* want her to stay here."

"What on earth are you driving at?"

Then, with even his indignation tired, he shrugged his shoulders and walked out of the room. It was true; they did not know what either of them meant; they had no points of contact, not even enough for an intelligible quarrel.

He drank his coffee in the surgery, and afterwards, as he went out for a few afternoon visits, the cloud of doubt and desperation suddenly

lifted when he passed Leni in the hall.   In her
smile he saw something that made him ex-
claim, eagerly: "Leni, the boy I told you about
last night — that case I said was hopeless — do
you remember?"

"Yes?"

"Well, it is n't — quite."

"Nothing 's hopeless, is it?"

He thought seriously for a moment: was it
really true that nothing was hopeless?   Then
he offered the result of his self-questioning.
"A few things, probably, but we don't know
what they are, thank heaven."

David had earned the reputation of being
absent-minded — something in his glance, perhaps, in the casual way he would begin and
end a chance conversation in the street, in the
way he walked and dressed, with the knot of
his tie always working looser and looser as the
day advanced; most of all, perhaps, in the
Legend of the Umbrella.   This legend dated
from 1902, from the service held in the Ca-

thedral to celebrate the end of the South African
War.   David and Jessica had walked up Shawgate, David smoking a pipe and Jessica carrying an umbrella; and just outside the Cathedral
porch, recollecting that he was about to enter
a sacred building, David had pressed down the
glowing tobacco and slipped the pipe, as he
thought, into his pocket.   But no; in the midst
of the service the umbrella, left in the stand
outside the pew, had begun to emit clouds of
smoke and, before anyone could attend to it,
burst into flame.   No harm was done, nothing
but a mild diversion caused, but the discovery
of the doctor's pipe in the wreckage had amused
Calderbury more than it had amused Jessica.

  After that we called the doctor absent-minded
and made jokes about the likelihood of his sew-
ing up sponges in a patient's body after an operation.   To anyone who ever saw him operate,
there could seem no risk of that.   But he did,
occasionally, forget appointments, and outside
his professional work there lay a misty territory
in which he could not be relied upon except for

good intentions. This business of helping
Leni to find a job was in just such territory.
His promises had been sincere enough, but he
had had no idea of the practical difficulties that
might lie ahead. The uncomfortable thing (to
him) was that she had to leave at all; not till
the second week of the fortnight did he suddenly realize that within a few days she might
find herself with nowhere else to go. Her arm
was still unfit for the strain of regular stage
dancing, even if any theatrical work had been
on offer; and he had innocently imagined that
in the last resort a knowledge of German would
easily secure her a post in some school. He was
surprised to find that so many other qualifica-
tions were required.

When, however, he returned to the house at
midday on the morning after the musical party,
Leni had news. A private school near Manchester was actually advertising for a part-time
teacher of German — "no diplomas necessary,
only a guaranteed ability to speak and teach
the language." David, perceiving no freakish-

ness in this, but simply common sense, was delighted; clearly it was just the thing. He even exclaimed: "Why, I go to Manchester now and again — I shall be able to look you up!"

All afternoon a warm feeling enveloped him which was really a childish dream that this business of Leni, himself, and Jessica might be settled with good will all round and to everyone's satisfaction: Leni in this new job, he himself seeing her from time to time, and Jessica — well, changing a little. It was n't that he wanted anything more of her — merely an absence of that silent hostility, that cold brooding of which he had lately become aware. So much of his life was beyond anything that she could touch; yet the part that was n't, though small, could fret the larger part, and did.

Leni wrote an application for the job, and David composed a testimonial for her to enclose with it. Then he went out to visit two or three cases. It was a hot day, glooming over with an approaching storm, and when he returned about four o'clock he went into the drawing-room because he saw it was cool with drawn blinds and also empty. Jessica's recent presence showed in a pile of letters on the bureau, addressed in her writing and waiting for the post. He might not have noticed them had not his sleeve, in passing, swept them over. Picking them up, he saw that one was addressed to the school near Manchester. Then Jessica entered, followed by Susan with the tea things, and he had the swift feeling that Jessica knew all about his having seen the address on that letter. He felt uneasy — partly, no doubt, his usual physical reaction to a storm. It was certainly coming. All day the heat wave had been lifting to a climax; the sky had grown opaque, like soiled muslin through which sunlight could barely strain. Then blackness began in a little patch and spread over half the sky. The storm broke while Jessica was pouring tea, and she said immediately: "David, please put the window up — we shall have all the tops of the curtains drenched."

He knew, or thought he knew, that she had

asked him to do this because he disliked going
near the window. It was not that he had any
bodily fear; it was from the look of doom in
the sky and from the sound of doom in the
thunderclaps that he shrank as from the sym-
bols of discord. He stood on the window seat
and braced himself for an eruption that seemed
due at any moment. It did not come, but the
tension held him miserably.

"I think you ought to know, David, I 've just
been writing a letter . . ."

He swung around. "You *have*? To that
school? About Leni?"

"You evidently have it on your mind. . . .
More tea?"

"N—no. . . . But why on earth should
you have written?"

"Well, *you* wrote, did n't you?"

"Only a testimonial."

"Don't you realize what that means?"

"Well, surely — "

"Do you realize that if she 's put in a
position of trust and betrays it you might

be held responsible for concealing the truth?"

"What truth? I only vouched for her character and knowledge of German."

"*Character?* Did you state that you met her first a few months ago, and that you did n't know a thing about her past life except that she 'd been on the stage and had tried to kill herself?"

"But — why — surely — "

"Well, I put it all in my letter in case you 'd forgotten."

"But — she may not get the job if you 've said all that."

"Is n't that *her* business? Why not try minding *ours* for a change?"

"Yes! Why not? That 's just it! Can't you leave the girl alone?"

"Can't *you?*"

Suddenly he realized that the letter was still there, unposted on the bureau. Striding over, he sought it hastily amidst the pile and tore it across. He was aware that the act was melodramatic, but all his nerves were craving for some if even the stupidest release in action.

"That just gives me the trouble of writing another. Really, David, you do the most childish things."

The room lit up with the tremendous flashing and roaring outburst that he had been expecting, yet was not and never could be prepared for. He saw Jessica's eyes gleaming at him across the hearthrug.

"And one more thing, David. I believe she sometimes comes in here to play the piano?"

"Yes, I said she could. After all, what harm does it do? She's really quite good at it — she ought to take it up seriously — "

"I don't wish her to play my piano in future, that's all."

"But there isn't any future! Good God, don't you realize that? In five days — "

"David, I think you'd better calm yourself."

"Yes, yes, I know — it's the storm, I think — I must get away — "

He rushed from the room and down the three steps, through the double doors into the surgery. It was far more dangerous there in a storm, for if a chimney stack were struck by lightning the débris would crash through the glass roof as through paper. But all he craved was the personal citadel where he could rest and be alone; and to be alone with Leni was still, in this deep sense, to be alone. There she was, arranging his papers, her upward glance a warm and welcoming thing.

"Please . . . is anything the matter?"

"I hate storms, Leni, that's all."

"It is nearly over now."

"Yes, I hope so. . . . I'm sorry to have to tell you . . . about that job . . ."

He told her all that had happened, ending with: "I tore it up, but I daresay she's written it again and posted it by now."

Suddenly it occurred to him that they were both children, acting and talking like children, with the same terrible intentness upon the hostile behavior of a grown-up.

"It means I won't get the job?"

"Probably not. But don't worry. I'll look

149

in at the Burrowsford Library to-morrow —
there may be some advertisements in scholastic
papers. The trouble is, as we've already
found, most of those posts go to people who
have degrees."

"Degrees?"

"What do you call them? I forget. Diploma? Baccalaureate? Doctorate?"

"Oh yes, I know."

An idea came to him, an offshoot of an already favorite idea. "Of course there's one
thing you really ought to do, especially if you
can't get a job."

"What's that?"

"Take up the piano seriously. There must
be a school somewhere you could join. Yes,
I'll look it up to-morrow in Burrowsford.
There's a conference there — I've got to attend. I hate things like that, but I'm on the
board of the County Hospital and it lets me in
for them now and again. Of course I could
lend you the money for the fees and you could
pay me back when you get a job again. . . .

Yes, that certainly *is* an idea. I'll find out all the details for you to-morrow. You see, there's an excellent reference library in Burrowsford — much better than here. . . . Perhaps the Academy of Music or something like that — in London, it might be. Maybe they offer scholarships and you could win one. I'll find out everything for you."

"But I'm not really a pianist, you know. I'm a dancer."

"Ah yes, of course. I was forgetting. Well, perhaps you could do that as well."

"Did you ever see the Russian Ballet?"

"I'm afraid not. In Calderbury, we hardly ever — "

"When I was in Petersburg — before I had to escape — I once saw Nijinsky."

It was plain that he had never heard of Nijinsky. He said, "Oh yes?"

"Would you like me to dance for you?"

He answered, with a touch of shyness: "Well, that would be very nice. I should certainly like it. But I don't quite see how — "

"Yet sometime, perhaps?"

"Yes, of course. Meanwhile I'll look up those advertisements for you. I still feel that it would be worth your while to take up the piano seriously — " And his mind ran easily on, as pleasantly unimpeded by practical knowledge as it usually was outside his own immediate world. And the following morning he went to the Burrowsford conference, which was just what he had expected it to be. Four days of listening to reports and speeches, of being chaffed by colleagues, of eating hotel meals — it was not the kind of life for which he had any social or temperamental aptitude. During his first day he found time to visit the library and spend an hour searching in a desultory way through year books and almanacs. He was one of those people who dislike asking expert advice, and, of course, as a professional dispenser of such advice, he was wholly inconsistent in this. He would have blamed a mother for not calling him in till too late, but he would not ask a library assistant how to look up details about entry into colleges of music. After much random searching he was fortunate enough to hit on the information he wanted; then he sat at one of the library desks and wrote as follows: —

DEAR LENI: I have looked into the matter we talked about. Of course I will give you full information when I return, but this is just to say that the idea of your taking up music at a college seems quite possible, and you can count on me for any help that is needed. Not a word to Jessie, though, or she might try to interfere — we must be careful not to make the same mistake as last time. . . .

When he had written as far as that, it occurred to him, in one of those spasms of caution that sometimes come to people who are not naturally cautious, that Jessica might even intercept the letter and read it; and to such a peril the only safeguard seemed to be transcription into deliberately vague terms. So he rewrote as follows: —

DEAR LENI: I have looked into the matter we were discussing yesterday, and I think the solution we thought of is the best, in the circumstances. Of course I will help you in it. All information and details when I return. Not a word to J. — we must be careful not to make the same mistake as last time — you know what I mean? So destroy this as soon as you have read it. . . .

When he had sealed and posted the letter he felt a sort of childish glee in having done something clever — he almost hoped that Jessica *would* intercept his message, since precious little she would learn from it, and that, in a way, would serve her right. He felt rather like a schoolboy who has invented some baffling stratagem against a strict but respected teacher.

Leni did not destroy the letter. It was the first she had ever received from him — the first time she had ever seen the words "Dear Leni" in his handwriting; and she kept it.

Three days later David reached Calderbury during the afternoon and walked from the station. There had been heavy rain and the Close was full of mixture scents, pebbles and bars of sand washed out of the gravel, pavements still steaming in the after-sun. And suddenly, as he walked past the Cathedral, the thought invaded him, as never before, of Leni. She would be there when he reached the house in Shawgate, but after that day and the next she would never be there again. He did not, because he could not somehow, think of the future without her, but all the sad urgency of the moment flowed back into the past, forcing him to remember the times they had met and talked, and how many more there could have been had he but known how soon they were all to end. "I have grown fond of that girl," he admitted to himself; and then, with a flash of self-blame, "Good heavens, four days at that confounded conference and now there's only one other day before she goes. . . ."

When he reached the house the interior seemed dark after the bright sunshine. It was Susan's half day off; Leni met him and said that Jessica was out also. "Would you like some tea?"

"That's just what I should like more than anything, Leni."

"Will you have it in the surgery?"

"That would be nice, too."

"All right. You look pale. Have you been very busy?"

"No, not busy — just bored. What have *you* been up to?"

"*Up to?* What does that mean?"

"What have you been *doing*?"

"Packing."

"Oh yes, of course."

And there, facing him again, was the imminence of her departure. He pondered on it as he sat alone and listened to the clatter of cups in the kitchen. Presently she reëntered, carrying a loaded tray.

"Seen the papers these last few days?" he asked.

She nodded.

"Looks bad, but I don't think it 'll come to anything over here."

156

"Come to anything?"

"Anything bad, I mean. But it's bad enough for those who are in it. Good thing you're not in your own country, perhaps. By the way, did you get my letter?"

"Yes, it was so good of you to write."

"Well, I thought you'd be relieved to know. About the music, I mean. It's a good idea . . . which reminds me, we can try over something this afternoon if you like — there's no one in — "

"But Mrs. Newcome said — "

"She'll never know."

"The people in the street will hear. Somebody will tell her."

"Then we'll close all the windows!" He added, boyishly: "Are you afraid?"

"Only for you, David."

"For me? Why, God bless my soul, what harm can come to me?"

She answered, in German: "You have to stay here after I have gone."

157

"I know. I'm trying to realize it. It's curious — I can't quite grasp the fact that you really *are* going and that this is your last day here. . . . I'll miss you. And really, I don't see why Jessie should forbid such a harmless thing."

So after the tea they went in the drawing-room and David stood on the window seat to close the windows. But one of them was stiff, and as he reached upwards to push, he lost balance and had to clutch a picture to save himself from falling. The picture came down on his head, showering him with dust; and of course he began to laugh, because he had a very simple and artless sense of humor. Then she went to the piano and he took out his violin and they began to play Mozart. The music streamed into the room, enclosing a world in which they were free as air, shutting out hatreds and jealousies and despondencies, giving their eyes a look of union with something rare and distant. David did not play very well — indeed, a good deal of the Mozart was much too difficult for him; but there was a simplicity that gave calmness to his effort, absorbing rather than interpreting the music. And he thought, as he played, that it was a strange thing, at forty-six, to know the sweetness and terror of existence as if one had never known them before, to look back mystically on the incredible chance of human contact, to feel some finger of destiny marking the streets of Calderbury where he had walked and talked with a girl.

When the last chord had been struck he began mumbling something about her playing being full of promise, and that she really ought to join some academy or *conservatoire*.

"You are so kind," she said.

"*Kind?* Why do you always say that?"

"Because you always say things like that, and you just say them because you are kind, that is all."

"But I mean them."

"I know.   But you don't mean them to mean anything."

"Now you 've puzzled me!" He smiled.

"Dear, I know why it is. You can't help it. And I love you — *I* can't help *that*."

But he was already bustling about saying, "Now I must put up that picture before anybody comes."

"You did n't hear me?"

"I 'm sorry . . . what was it?"

She said, smiling: "I know. There is just one thing more. I will dance for you."

"Dance for me? Here? *Now?*"

"Yes. You know the prelude of Chopin that goes like this — " she hummed a few bars of it. "You play that on your violin — I will dance to it."

"But — "

"Yes? You are afraid if anybody comes? You are afraid if anyone sees through the window? Pull over the curtains. Take up the rugs. . . . Please do that until I come back. . . ."

She ran out of the room and was away a few minutes. During this interval David waited

indecisively at first, then, with a sudden clinch-
ing of intention, did as she had asked. First
the curtains, then the rugs. The room filled
with a warm twilight; he did not switch on any
lights because the sunshine out of doors came
through the fabric of the curtains in a luminous
glow. Then he took his violin and tried over,
very softly, the prelude she had mentioned.

Presently she came into the room, dressed
in a ballet costume that bore, if he had noticed
it, the creases of repeated packings and unpack-
ings. Had he noticed, too, he would have
seen that it was a little shabby, and had never
been anything remarkable even when new.
But in the twilight he saw nothing but a strange
vision of the mind, something he had never expected to see in this life, an embodiment of
light and air, on tiptoe with a dream. He took
up his violin and began to play, watching her
all the time. She was magic to him. There
was something between them pouring always
in invisible streams, the awareness of beauty
in peril.

So on an August afternoon, behind drawn curtains in a Calderbury drawing-room, a girl danced for the little doctor. The room filled with the emptiness of all the world except themselves, and this emptiness soared in their hearts until, just on the edge of flight, the spell was broken by the ringing of the telephone.

David put down his violin. Leni stopped still. "A call for me probably," he said, beginning to walk away. Leni more slowly followed. A moment later he was finding his bag and hat in the surgery.

"That boy, you know — the pneumonia case — I have to go at once."

"And I must change and finish packing. I 'll tidy the room up too."

"Thanks. . . . Maybe I 'll be back soon." And he added, gently: "It was very beautiful."

Ten minutes later he was in the familiar strangeness of rooms and stairs. There could be no doubt about the case this time.

He sat by the bedside, taking a small hand in

his own, and the boy, half conscious as he fought for breath, looked up and smiled. Suddenly — almost immediately — death came. Weeks afterwards the boy's father, in the four-ale bar of the "Greyhound," described the incident. "He killed our Johnny, too. Pewmonia, Johnny had, double pewmonia, and Newcome had bin to see him several times but never done the boy no good. And it was that night — *that* night, mind you. Maybe he was thinkin' about it all the time he was with our Johnny. Because what d' you think he did when he got to the boy? Why, nothing. Just sat there and let the poor kid die without so much as raising a finger! The dirty swine!"

We do not know what to-night, much less to-night's newspaper, will bring. Some secret intersection of seconds and inches may mean an end to us, our age, the world. In Calderbury on that evening of August fourth, the train brought in later editions from Marsland, catching the sunset on its windows so that a flash of crimson streaked the water meadows. In the streets of the town the newspapers were scrambled for, and one of them by the little doctor, who stood reading it as he held his bicycle at the curb.

"Looks bad, doctor," someone said.

"Yes, indeed. Good God, I never thought they'd actually come to it!"

"Soon over, you bet. Wait till the Navy — "

Half listening, he read paragraphs about mobilizations, troops rushed to frontiers, bombardments opened on fortifications, refugees streaming from ravaged lands, the plight of travelers and aliens. Abruptly then he moved off along Briargate, pedaling faster than usual, till he was hot and breathless. He entered the house through the surgery, leaving the bicycle against the wall in the outside alley. Mechanically he unlocked a cupboard to replace some drugs he had carried with him in his bag. He could feel his heart pounding with excitement as he climbed the stairs to the attic room where he

guessed Leni would be waiting. He was that
strange creature, a quiet man resolved upon
an act. The trouble was that life with Jessica
had given him this curious reluctance, outside
his own world, to make decisions; she had
made so many for him, and her intolerance of
most that he dared to contemplate himself had
blanketed him with at least a vagueness and at
most an obstinacy. Only in his own world was
there freedom of mind and hand; and in that
world he had been eager to imprison himself
for such freedom. He had never bothered
much about exterior events. He had found
contentment within the circle of a few things
he cared for, and outside it he walked as a
child.

But now, having suddenly made up his mind,
he was in a tremendous hurry. He must act.
He must even oppose Jessica, if need be —
must use decision, cunning, worldly wisdom,
a host of qualities strange to him. "Leni, my
dear — you can't wait till to-morrow — you've
got to get away now — to-night!"

She was kneeling on the floor of the attic room, packing clothes into a bag.

"But — why?"

"It's in the paper. England and Germany may be at war by midnight. That means you must get away. You *must* go back — to Germany — at once — before anything can happen — "

"But I can't — I — "

"I tell you you must get out of England — somewhere — anywhere. Don't you realize what it'll be like if you stay? Already they're arresting and imprisoning people. Hurry now and finish packing — we have to leave at once."

"*We?*"

"Of course. I'm going to help you. We've missed the last train, but there's one from Marsland that goes at ten to twelve — we can get there somehow — "

"*We?*"

"Yes, yes — I'm going to take you to a seaport and arrange for you to get away in time — so hurry, please hurry. . . ." And so he talked on. She did n't want to go and finally she was hysterical. He calmed her and after about an hour they went downstairs and through the surgery into the narrow path flanked by the white sea shells. There the sight of his bicycle leaning against the wall gave him both confidence and a new access of caution. "You must n't be seen leaving the town, especially with me, so this is what we must do. . . . Now let me think — it 's almost dusk — you take the path to the Knoll and wait for me by the wooden hut — you remember it? We 'll meet there and go on — I 'll take the long way round by the lane — "

She hesitated a moment, then nodded. As soon as she had gone, the path between the high walls seemed an empty canyon, and in his own heart an equal emptiness gave answer. He must help her out of the country. He must *act*. He must be forceful and yet remain calm. So he waited to light his pipe, waited after that for a whole minute by his watch, and then, wheeling the bicycle, emerged into the street.

Through the quiet streets off Briargate and into Lissington Lane the little doctor hastened, full of the strange sensation of having decided to do something at last. He thought he was clever to have arranged to meet Leni at the wooden hut, because it was dark there, and no one would see their faces. And it was clever of him also, he thought, to have arranged separate journeys to the rendezvous, for while no one would think much of seeing either of them alone, the pair of them might be (indeed, in the past, had been) gossiped about. So he cycled along, slowly because of the steepness, making a short cut to the edge of the town, where, a little way along the lane, a field path led to the Knoll. He would have to wheel his bicycle there, along the zigzag path over the quarry, and so to the wooden hut in the dark part of the woods.

Even in Calderbury streets he hoped that no one would notice him, and he pulled his hat well down over his eyes with some vague idea of disguising himself. But after almost colliding with another cyclist he gave this up as impracticable; besides, a few people saw him, anyway, calling to him out of windows and doorways as he went by: "Good night, doctor. . . . Heard the news, I suppose?" — to which, because he could not think of anything else and also because he was incapable of not returning cordiality, he answered in a strained voice: "Good night, Jim . . . yes. . . . Good night, Dick. . . . Good night, Mrs. Hargreaves." Once, at a street corner, he overheard a man telling a small group of people: "There's a big battle going on in the North Sea — our Tom heard it from the telephone exchange. The German fleet is sinking. . . ."

Presently he came to the field path. It was a lovely night, warm from the earth; and he felt, as he always did when he had seen recent death, a mystic communion with all things living and dead, as well as a perception of their own communion; so that, through such a prism of consciousness, he could sense life in a dead stone and death in a living tree. As he came to the edge of the disused quarry he happened to kick a pebble and heard it fall a hundred feet to the rocks and undergrowth at the base of the cliff. Perhaps the universe had been made as chancily as that.

Soon, through the trees, he saw the shape of the wooden hut, and beside it, waiting for him, Leni. He could not see her clearly, but as he approached she came to him, and they stood for a moment, searching each other's eyes till light was born in them, and it seemed to him then that the universe might even more probably have been made like *that*.

"Have you been waiting long?"

"About ten minutes. I did n't mind."

"We must move on. Did anyone see you?"

"I don't think so."

"It does n't really matter, I suppose, once we 've got away."

They descended the Knoll by a path that led them to the other side of it, whence, at the foot, the water meadows stretched to the Marsland Road. The night was pale over those meadows, and only the sudden lighting of cigarettes marked pairs of lovers couched in the long grasses; there was no sound but secret voices under the mist and the hum of the bicycle as David pushed it. He was hoisting it over the last stile when the Cathedral chimed the three quarters. "Now we're all right," he said, stooping to light the lamp when they reached the highway. Warm dust-scented air lingered over the graveled road. "Have you ever ridden on the back of a bicycle? You'll find it quite easy. Put your left foot on the axle step and your right knee on the mudguard — you'll manage."

So they began the journey from Calderbury, with the lamplight flickering and swerving as David pedaled along. The road lay slightly uphill, and it was hard work; but there was no traffic as there would be to-day, no speeding cars, no young men with motorcycles racing between the hedges, no huge omnibuses linking the villages at forty miles an hour; only an old man plodding home, who called "Good night" without knowing, without even trying to see, who passed him. And presently the moon rose and the twin towers of the Cathedral stiffened against the blue-black sky, calling eleven as David topped the hill and prepared to freewheel down. The hill heaped behind, with the dark shape of the Knoll farther still behind, the gradient spinning them into shadows of cold air under trees, and then into the bright glassy moonlight of the level. And after miles of this, keeping a good rate, David began to whistle in pure enjoyment. He often did so as he went about the countryside at night, and if people heard a whistling cyclist they sometimes said: "Bet you that's the little doctor." So now he went on whistling till the beginning of Croombury Hill made him save his breath, and a few yards higher forced him off his machine altogether. He dismounted with the usual acrobatic flourish for which Leni was hardly prepared and which would have capsized her into the ditch had she not been agile.

"This is a steep one," he said, affectionately, to the earth and sky, and then paused in the middle of the road, feeling in his pocket for pipe and tobacco and matches. "But we're doing fine — we'll easily catch the ten to twelve. Are you tired?"

"No, but it hurts my knee a little."

"It's not far now — just through Lissington village and over the next hill. I know all the country round here. Every village and lane and path. I know the people in the cottages, and in the churchyards too. This is a good country, England. I've been round about here for fifteen years. You must have been a baby when I first put up my plate. Hundreds of miles away in some German village I've never heard of, and you grew up — all unknown to me, all those years — to fall over one night and break your wrist in Calderbury. If you hadn't come here and done that I'd never have known you at all. That's a funny thing. And it's funnier still to think that I should n't have missed knowing you. . . . Some German village, was n't it? Tell me about it."

"It was a city, really — Königsberg. My parents both died when I was young and I was sent to a school — the school I ran away from."

"We 're at the top of the hill now. Better jump on again. We can go on talking."

He kept his cherry-wood pipe in his mouth and the smoke and sometimes the flakes of hot tobacco flew back in her face as they gathered speed. "Plenty of time," he muttered, wobbling dangerously as he pointed to the horizon. "There are the Junction lights — see them? That reddish glow yonder!"

But at the foot of the hill there was a bad patch in the road and crossing it too fast and with the added weight the back tire suddenly deflated. David braked with a vehemence that nearly threw Leni forward over his head. "Oh dear, that's really a nuisance," he said, contemplatively, coming to a standstill and viewing the rear wheel. "We 'll just have to push on and walk. Plenty of time if we hurry a bit." He wheeled the machine for a little way, then it occurred to him that it was no help and that they would gain time by leaving it. He took it through a gate into a field and partly hid it in a hedgerow.

They went on again, but Leni was limping from her right knee; she could not walk very fast, and the Junction lights seemed far away. He put his arm round her so that she might lean some of her weight on him. A little wood came slowly towards them on the left, snuffing out the roadway and changing the sound of their footsteps. From the distance came the clank of wagons in the shunting yard, and an owl mournfully replied from the little wood near by. They both laughed at that. But when they entered the moonlight again the horizon glow looked no nearer. "Just a matter of stepping out," he said, but they could not easily increase their pace. And when, still a long way off, they heard the train they had aimed for puffing out of the station, it was almost a relief to slacken, to sit on a stile while David smoked a pipe, to talk intermittently and catch the tiny friendly sounds of a twig snapping or a dog barking distinctly.

An early morning train left Marsland at six-five, and David thought it would probably connect with other trains so that they could reach the coast by afternoon. They had six hours to wait — no big hardship on a summer night. Half a mile further on he knew that the side of the road heaped into a dry bed of bracken; sometimes, cycling around, he had paused there for a few minutes' rest. It was a place called Potts Corner, though why and who Potts was nobody knew. But there was a big elm growing there, and a signpost marking a field path to Stamford Magna.

So when they were tired of talking they walked to the Corner and lay down on the turf and bracken. There are some moments that are hung in memory like a lamp; they shine and swing gently and one can look back on them when all else has faded into distance and darkness. Often afterwards David remembered that roadside corner and the hours he spent there; and sometimes he thought of things he would like to have said and done while there was yet a chance; but actually he said and did very little, because he was tired, and with tiredness had come an old familiar inability to make up his mind. Presently, with his arms round her, she fell asleep. A little wind stirred in the elm overhead; the air grew chilly as the night advanced. He began to wish he had brought an overcoat. For that matter he wished he had brought food, and far more money than was in his pockets; and then he reflected how bad he really was at planning these things, and how much more efficient Jessica would have been. And also he remembered Leni's own carelessness of detail when she had tried to take her life at Sandmouth; strange that he should be showing such similar lack of forethought in his efforts to save it. And then he began to feel sleepy himself.

Dawn came — the dawn of that first day of war. He got up, leaving her still sleeping, and walked a few yards to the signpost.

"Stamford Magna, 2 miles." To peace, how many days, months, years? He lit a pipe and watched the dawn turn to sunrise. The spire of Lissington Church pricked over the lightening horizon; day came rolling over the little hills, filling the sunken roadways, glistening on the wheat fields, wakening the birds. A harness jingled in some far stable. In a little while it would be time to walk to the Junction, where he had remembered there were chocolate slot machines. Then later, when they reached some bigger place, they could have a real breakfast.

He roused her and they passed on together, facing the early morning sunlight. Soon the road entered the long level stretch at the end of which could be seen the station buildings and a signal tower. It was ten to six when they approached the entrance to the ticket office and David had another of those precautionary ideas that only occur to people who are not really good at precautions — it suddenly occurred to him that at the station everybody knew him

well and that it would be safer to slip on to the
platform through the shunting yard and board
the train without taking tickets. This he did,
easily enough, for the train was already drawn
up at the platform and there was ample choice
of unoccupied compartments. He knew that
the train would take them as far as Charlham,
where they could buy the tickets and pick up
an express to London.

Feeling rather pleased with this excellent
strategy, he smoked contentedly while Leni
settled into the cushions and went to sleep
again. He was still thinking how cleverly he
had escaped being recognized by the station
staff when he recollected the chocolate in the
slot machines; and he was just wondering
whether he could risk a last-minute dash across
the platform when, at the same last minute,
the door of the compartment opened and a
man, paunchy, middle-aged, and breathless,
jumped in and flung himself down in the
corner seat opposite David. "Why," he began,
"if it is n't Dr. Newcome — well — *well?* . . .

Remember the last time we traveled on this line, doc? Too warm for gloves this weather, eh?" He began to laugh and chuckle, and David smiled ruefully and could n't help saying, as he might have done in the surgery: "You should n't run for trains, Barney, at your age. It's the worst heart strain you can think of, because it's excitement as well as physical effort—"

Later, some time later, months later in fact, Barney Tinsley confessed that he had not at first realized that the girl in the other corner was traveling with the doctor. She had been asleep, and he was surprised when she suddenly woke up and said something in a foreign language. Well, more than surprised—regular flabbergasted.

The gloves allusion was explained to a different audience as follows. "Did I ever tell you, gents, about that time I was in the train with him going to Sandmouth? Y' know, it's funny, the way you remember things. . . . Well, thanks, sir, that's very kind of you. Well, I was sort of dozing off, y' know, the same as you do in trains, when suddenly the doc stumbles over my feet, waking me up sudden, and I see him deliberately throw one of his gloves out of the window. 'Goodness, is the fellow crazy?' I sez to myself, for it was a good glove, by the look of it, real kid. Course I asked him what the idea was, and I 'll take a bet none of you fellers can't guess the answer. . . . I thought it would stump you — stumped me at the time. I 'll tell you what he sez to me — 'Barney,' he sez, — he always called me Barney, — 'I just dropped a glove accidental on the line as I was opening the window, and I thought I might as well throw the other one after it, so as maybe the same person would find 'em both. After all, an odd glove's not much use to anybody, is it?' Must 'ave had a queer mind to think of things as quick as that. . . ."

"Queer is the word," somebody responded.

They arrived at Charlham at nine-thirty and had breakfast in the Railway Arms. The morning papers had just come, and everyone in the coffee room was talking and prophesying — the waiter, a few commercial travelers, and a man in a green baize apron who was cleaning the fireplace. The bacon was cold and the toast burnt. David had looked up the time-table and found an express to London at eleven; the station was just across the road, so there was plenty of time. He left Leni in the hotel lounge while he found a barber's shop and had a shave.

Most of the way to London she slept again, but this time the train was crowded and she leaned her head against his shoulder while he talked with the other people in the compart-ment. That always happened wherever he went; people always began talking to him, tell-ing him all their lives if there were time enough, because he had a way of listening gently. But this time, as he talked and listened, he some-times stole a glance at the head so limp against his arm; it had been a long way to the Junction for her — poor child, let her sleep. But once she half-wakened, roused by the crash of the

train into a tunnel, and in the sudden soft glow
of the electric light her eyes melted to his glance.
"Du kleiner Doktor . . ." she murmured,
dreamily. "Where are we going to? Where
are you taking me?" Then she remembered
something he had told her — that she must not
speak during the journey in case anyone should
hear her foreign accent.

They reached London in the middle of the
afternoon, and as they walked with the crowd
on the platform by the side of the train two
men sprang forward and gripped each of them
by the arm.

CHAPTER VI

THE little doctor watched the autumn sunlight move over the floor, and when the
last yellow bar disappeared he knew it was late
afternoon and that another day was nearly over.
Presently he heard the Cathedral chiming five,
and a warder entered with tea and bread and
butter for himself and for the other two warders who had to stay all the time. According
to prison rules he was never left alone, day or
night; but the warders were kindly fellows
and tried to efface themselves as much as possible. They played cards or read newspapers
or yarned together for hours, not worrying the
doctor by their presence, though they were af-
fable enough if he chose to join them for a game

or a chat. Of course he already knew and called them by their first names. "It's a queer thing, George," he said (and this was the thing George quoted oftenest afterwards), "I can't seem to get used to wearing boots without bootlaces. You'd think it would be more comfortable, really, but somehow it is n't."

They would not let him wear bootlaces, or braces, or anything he might possibly hang himself with; because, of course, they intended to hang him themselves.

But in other ways he was treated with consideration; indeed, as he told the Governor whenever the latter visited him, "I'm quite comfortable, thank you." He could smoke, read books and newspapers, and have any kind of food he fancied. And as Calderbury Prison was mostly disused, the part he occupied was not in the original cell block at all, but consisted of a couple of ordinary rooms with nothing unusual about them except steel locks on the doors and bars to the windows. Only a little less comfortable than the rooms he

occupied in his own house in Shawgate, for he
had never had luxurious tastes. In some ways
he was almost freer than he had been at home;
for he could get up and go to bed when he
liked and he had ample leisure to read. Everyone in Calderbury Prison was sorry for the
little doctor and rather embarrassed because in
three weeks' time he was to die. After the dismissal of the appeal the Governor was almost
apologetic when he brought the news. " 'Fraid
I've nothing good to tell you, Newcome —
still, I know you had n't been counting on
it. . . . And remember, anything I can do
now . . . you must n't mind telling me."

"There's only one thing — you remember
I asked you before."

"Oh, *that?* Well . . . I can only say again
I wish I could, but it's dead against all the reg-
ulations. Just the one thing I *can't* do for you.
I 'm sorry."

The request that David had made, more than
once, was to see Leni. She was lodged in the

jail at Midchester, twenty miles away, where there was more up-to-date provision for women prisoners. He had not seen her since the trial a month before, and when he tried to remember that last glance he had he could only see the courtroom, dark at the close of an autumn afternoon, grey figures moving restlessly and meaninglessly as reeds in a stream, and somewhere, lost amongst them, her strange eager face seeking his in a bewildered stare. What had it all been about? And he did n't know — the whole proceedings of arrest, police questioning, grand jury, prison, trial . . . all were shadows of a shapeless fate. They let him read newspaper reports of the trial, and to these he now gave a half-incredulous scrutiny. He could not really understand. Then he turned to the current papers and read news that was dark with huger fantasy — Mons, the Marne, the Aisne. . . .

He found it tolerable at first to watch the days crawl by. He was not afraid of death; he knew that death could be prophesied for all men; he had often prophesied it himself. Even to look ahead and know that a month hence he would lie in a prison grave was no worse than to diagnose, as many a doctor must, the first budding in his own flesh that will bring death as its flower. And the routine of prison helped to a certain tranquillity; in the mornings when he took exercise in the graveled yard he smiled at the sky and let the wind blow lovingly through his hair. It had gone grey during recent months, but they had not made him clip it short.

In the afternoons he read or rested or played a game of cards with the two men on guard over him, and soon after tea, because there was nothing else to do, he went to bed. It was nighttime that was the worst. He could not sleep well between midnight and dawn; and then, in those guardless hours (for the warders, against rules, usually dozed off themselves), he thought of Leni. Love is a strange thing; we may not notice the moment it comes, yet there is a moment when we know it is there —

sudden wakefulness, as to pleasure or pain after sleep, a sudden color, as of a painting after an etching. So it had been for the little doctor; he remembered a moment in the courtroom, during the judge's summing up; he had been tired after a long day in that stuffy atmosphere, and the judge's words had droned on more and more slowly, as if they were being pushed into sound by means of an ever greater effort. A little way off in the prisoner's dock Leni was sitting, and she too looked tired, had lapsed into a remoteness that seemed, by its very detachment from environment, an almost physical absence. The judge was going over the points of the case, one by one; and presently he said: —

". . . With evidence of motive, gentlemen, we are not primarily concerned when there is so much suggestive evidence as to fact . . . but . . . you will probably conjecture the purpose for which he brought her from Sandmouth to Calderbury, and you will form your own opinion as to the validity of the pretext of

189

engaging her as his young son's governess. It may well be that you will feel that no more unsuitable person could have been chosen to look after a nine-year-old child — and a very nervous and highly strung child, we have been told — than a young woman whose temperament was such that she had only recently attempted suicide, who had had no kind of previous experience as a child's governess, and who, in addition, could barely make herself understood in the child's language. . . . You will have to ask yourselves, plainly and straightforwardly, what lay behind this extraordinary incident — doubtless it can be made to look attractive if you think of it in terms of rescue and benevolence, but if you will bear in mind the culmination to which it led, and which is the sole cause of our being here to-day to pass judgment, then you will form your own opinion why the prisoner chose to install this young woman in the very centre of his household, where he could see her every day and as often and for as long periods as he liked, and where,

under the same roof as his wife and son . . .
Gentlemen, it is, of course, for you to decide
and interpret these matters so far as you feel
justified in doing so — I only desire to caution
you against the pseudo or false romanticism of
which plays and novels are such frequent ex-
ponents — the kind, I mean, that deal with
what I believe is called the 'eternal triangle.'
Such fair words are, in a measure, hypocritical;
they may lull us for an evening's entertain-
ment, but in a court of law it is our duty to
remember — and it is my duty to point out —
the plainer and less agreeable facts . . . lust
. . . infatuation . . . the lowest and basest
physicality, uncontrolled, dominating . . . all
of which, gentlemen, is apt, in our modern
world, as you know, to be loosely summed up
under the word 'love.'   You may call it 'love'
if you like, provided you realize . . ."

And at that the whole mumbling greyness
seemed to be lit by a stabbing trumpeting light;
and the little doctor said in his heart, almost
as if he were taking advantage of permission

just given him: "Yes, I call it love.". . . It was so wrong, absurd, preposterous, all that the judge had said; and yet, just round the corner from the nonsense, there was this imperishable pearl of truth. "I call it love. Oh God, yes. I call it love."

Looking back as he tried to sleep during those last nights in Calderbury Jail, the little doctor sighed only because that moment had happened so late. And thence, inevitably, he turned to thinking of love that had always been in his heart, and in the hearts of so many: love of mankind that had sheltered long in the monk's cell and the artist's studio and the doctor's laboratory; love that had made men quietly build and sacrifice and die; love that might have conquered the world had not its moment arrived too late.

Chimes of the Cathedral marked the quarters, marked the slow tragedy of that lateness, while the little doctor dreamed, remembering the millions crouched in their trenches . . . hate, murder, agony . . . the lowest and basest, uncontrolled, dominating . . . all of which, gentlemen, is apt, in our modern world, to be loosely summed up under the word "love." You may call it love if you like, provided you realize . . . and then he fell asleep for a few troubled moments, waking again, and half-sleeping again, until the dawn outlined the bars across the window. They call it love, I call it love, but we do not mean the same thing.

To his dying day (which was, in fact, the day after) the little doctor never knew why it was that the prison authorities allowed him to see Leni. The reason is disclosed in a book published only a few years ago by Major Sir George Millman under the somewhat catch-penny title *My Forty Years in Jail*. There is a paragraph of interesting reminiscence about the Calderbury case: —

Newcome was under my charge both before and after sentence; he was a quiet fellow on the whole, and gave very little trouble. The only request he persistently made was to see his co-prisoner, Fräulein

Leni Krafft, who had shared his conviction and sentence and was imprisoned a few miles away. Of course, as I told him, this was altogether contrary to regulations, but I happened to mention his request to Sir William Clintock, who was in charge of the wartime secret service, and he took it up from another angle. It seemed that very little was known about the German girl, apart from the Calderbury case; but a forged passport was discovered amongst her possessions after her arrest, and the espionage department suspected that she was a German spy who had earlier been working in Russia. Of course all this was kept out of the court evidence, and it did not affect the question of her guilt in the Calderbury charge. Sir William, however, believed that a last-minute interview with Newcome might reveal some hint as to her real identity and perhaps afford clues that would assist the Department in countering the machinations of enemy espionage; so after consultation with the Home Office permission was duly given and the two condemned prisoners talked for half an hour in a room in Calderbury Jail which they had been encouraged to think was private. Actually several persons, including one who knew German perfectly, were listening and taking notes all the time, through holes that had been made secretly

in the paneling of the room. The idea was un-
doubtedly worth trying out, but in point of fact the
two prisoners exchanged no remarks that were of any
help to the Department.

When David heard on Thursday morning
that his one request had been granted and that
Leni was to be brought to see him that same
afternoon, his heart overflowed with anticipation and he pressed the Governor's hand with
more emotion than he had yet shown since his
arrival at the jail. The Governor was a little
embarrassed. "Not at all . . . not at all,
Newcome . . . don't thank me — thank the
authorities. Still, I 'm jolly glad for your sake.
Anything else I can do, y' know. . . ."

"How long can we talk for?"

"Oh well . . . no exact time limit, y' know
. . . pretty well as long as you like within
reason. Say half an hour. Plenty of time for
anything you want to say to each other. We
shan't bother you."

"You mean there 'll be nobody listening?"

"Maybe we 'll stretch a point and call the

warders off. . . . I daresay you'd like it better in private. Oh, and by the way . . ."

"Yes?"

"You remember at the trial — right at the
end — you told the judge that the girl was
really only nineteen — "

"Yes. But he would n't listen to me."

"I know. I'm interested, all the same, in
what you said. Did you only just say it to try
to get her off?"

"No, it was true."

"But how did you know it was true? What
reason had you for thinking her so young?"

"She told me."

"Oh, I see. . . . You had n't any evidence
except just that?"

"I believed her."

"Yes, of course. . . . Ah well, you'll see
her this afternoon."

And a few minutes later, recovering from his
embarrassment, Millman telephoned to the
Governor of Midchester Prison. "Yes, I told
him it would be private. Did you tell *her* the

same? Good . . . rather an awkward business, really. . . . Oh Lord, no, he was so
damn pleased about it — thought I'd fixed it
as a special favor, y'know. Rather pathetic,
in a way . . . made me feel a bit of a . . . oh
yes, I asked him about the girl's age, but he
knew nothing definite — only that she'd told
him she was only nineteen. Seems to have
believed everything she told him, poor devil.
. . . Yes, all right — three o'clock. We've
fixed the room and the men will be ready. . . ."

At five to three the little doctor was taken
along corridors to a room he had never seen
before, a small match-boarded room in which
were a table and two chairs. He sat down on
one of the chairs and a warder took the other.
Then at a few minutes after the hour another
warder made some signal from the door, at
which the first warder got up and left the
room. For a few seconds David was alone;
then the door opened, and Leni, also alone,
entered.

They had let her come in ordinary clothes,

the same that she had worn whilst balancing on the back of David's bicycle along the Marsland Road. But her face was different from then; she had the little crushed smile that he had seen first of all when he had bandaged her wrist after the accident at the Theatre Royal. She came forward, stumbling a little, leaning at last into his arms as he stood. *"Du kleiner Doktor . . . Oh, du kleiner Doktor. . . ."* She began to cry, and all at once it seemed to him that the whole world was crying, crying for lost, impossible love.

Her first words were: "David, whatever you did, I love you, David. I told you that once before, but you took no notice."

"When did you tell me?"

"That day I danced for you."

"Yes, I remember that. I try to remember everything — I try and I try — but I can't think what really happened. Perhaps nobody knows what happened." And then suddenly he said: "Leni — did you — you did n't — you did n't — do anything — did you?"

She looked at him gravely for a moment and then answered: "No.   Did *you?*"

"I did n't either.   Did you think I did?"

"I wondered."

"I wondered too."   Then he smiled.   "Forgive me.   How could such a suspicion — "

"But if it 's really true that neither of us — "

"Yes?"

"Then *who?*"

"Yes, that 's the trouble.   That 's why they won't believe us.   They have to find some answer.   They have to blame somebody.   And it 's so easy to prove things by evidence."

She put up her hand and touched his face as a blind person memorizes.   "They are going to kill us, David, though we have n't done any wrong at all."

"I know."   And he added, seeing beyond her, hundreds of miles beyond her: *"We are not alone."*

"What do you mean?"

"These things are always happening.   Don't

be afraid of death. It is n't the worst we have to face — only the last."

"But that is why it *is* the worst."

"No, no, we should fear birth far more if we could look ahead to it." And then, half-impishly, he began to improvise on the theme, to play with the idea for her comfort and his own. "Oh, much more, I assure you. I 've often thought that. Suppose, just for argument, that everything *did* happen the other way round. Suppose people gathered in a churchyard and hauled you from a hole in the ground in a wooden box and took you back to a house, and after a day or so the box was opened and you were laid on a bed, and a few days later people gathered at the bedside and all at once the breath of life came into you, bringing agony first of all, then less and less till you could actually stir and creep about, walking with a stick perhaps and being for a time a bit deaf and blind and crazy . . ."

"Horrible!"

"But not nearly as horrible as when you come

to the other end. For think of the day you'd
leave school and begin to stay at home in the
nursery. Think of the first time you'd really
believe in Santa Claus and hang up your stocking on Christmas Eve! Think of people pat-
ting you on the head as you grew younger every
day, as you gradually lost speech and height and
weight and personality! That last stumbling
walk across the hearthrug before you settled
down to pram life! How unutterably tragic
— far more so than growing old and dying!"

"But — never — *never* — to see you again!"

"Maybe you will. If there's a next world
I'll try to find you in it as I found you in this.
There will be other worlds, surely, or maybe
this world over again . . . worlds in which
the things we have won't be wasted like this.
. . . I'll find you . . . do you remember
that first night I *did* find you? Very windy
— later on it rained. First of all I went to
the theatre, and you'd gone. But I found you
in the end."

" — I saw you through the mirror as you

came into the room, and I knew you must be the little doctor because you looked so . . . you looked so . . . Oh, David — *David!* . . . *Why* does it have to happen like this?"

Afterwards, while Leni was hastening back to Midchester in a car with drawn blinds, the listeners in the next room compared notes. It was generally admitted that the interview had been a failure.

"Of course it was pretty obvious he smelt a rat. Did n't you hear him whisper 'We 're not alone'? That was a hint to her to be careful what she said. . . . It 's my belief Millman gave the game away talking to him beforehand. Not too subtle, the Major, compared with the old doc — *he 's* got his head screwed on all right —"

"Till to-morrow morning," somebody answered with a nervous smile, for hanging is really no joke.

Twilight ushered in the evening, and David watched the slow glooming of the sky with

full awareness that it was for the last time.
He was not unhappy. He was not afraid.
He was quite calm when the Governor and
the Chaplain paid the formal visits that were
part of enjoined routine.

The Chaplain came first, a jolly-looking red-
faced parson chosen for the job of ministering
to the spiritual needs of prisoners because it
was supposed that he knew how to deal with
men, could meet them on their own level, and
so on. His sermons were always full of pat-
you-on-the-back optimism, and he said "damn"
just to prove his good fellowship. He had
known Jessica, through her connection with
the Cathedral clergy, and she had always regarded him as "just the kind of parson the
modern world needs." All of which might
have made him embarrassed to meet David,
had he not been the kind of man who is rarely
embarrassed. He sat on the edge of the bed
and beamed with man-to-mannishness. "Comfortable, eh, Newcome? Having all you
want?"

"Yes, thank you," said David, who always filled in gaps of emotional response by being polite.

"Thought you might care for a little chat, y' know. How 're you feeling? All right? Pretty cheerful? Read the papers, I suppose? Damned awful thing if the boys are n't home by Christmas, eh? Still, it can't be long after — we 've certainly got the enemy by the short hairs — "

Suddenly David realized who this man was. "Why, you knew Jessie, did n't you?" he interrupted.

Even the Chaplain's nerve was somewhat unprepared for the shock of such a reference. "You mean — you mean — Mrs. — the late Mrs. Newcome? Why, yes, I did know her — yes, of course I did." (As he said to Millman afterwards: "You could have knocked me down with a feather when he mentioned her — so damn casual, you would n't believe it possible. . . .")

Then David began to talk quite normally —

that is to say, from the Chaplain's point of view, quite abnormally. "I'm glad to speak to someone who knew her, because you'll understand about Gerald — that's my boy. Jessie had sent him away to her brother-in-law — Simpson, you know, he's the Vicar of St. Peter's. I'm sure he's being looked after all right, but I do hope they haven't told him — very much — you know what I mean — you see he's so nervous — "

"My dear Newcome, you needn't worry on that score. I happen to know that your boy's been told *nothing* — absolutely nothing. As a matter of fact he's at present away at the seaside — much the best idea, don't you think? I suppose some day . . . but for the present — well, he just thinks his mother and father have gone away somewhere for a time. . . . Of course if you'd put in an application I've no doubt they'd have allowed you to see him — but all the same — "

"Oh, I never thought of it — oh, dear no. I wouldn't like him to come here at all — he'd

be frightened — he was always scared of police-
men. I think that was because Jessie always
used to say, 'I'll fetch a policeman to you,'
whenever he misbehaved — a mistake to say
things like that to a nervous child. And that's
what I want to talk to you about. . . . You
know Jessie meant well, but she didn't really
understand the boy. She and I had different
ways with him, and I think — I really *do* think
— mine was better. I wish you'd tell the
Simpsons that if you get the chance. Tell
them not to worry the boy, just let him grow
up and conquer things for himself . . . and
then some day, maybe, he can know the truth
about me — about — *to-morrow,* I mean. . . ."

"Well, Newcome, I must say I think that's
very sensible of you. You can rest assured I'll
do my damnedest for the youngster. Keep
an eye on him myself, I give you my word.
As 'matter of fact, if I had my way I'd
tell him a complete lie about you — I'd say
you'd joined up and made the — er — the
supreme sacrifice — give the little chap some-

thing to be proud of. . . . Why not — eh, why not?"

And then the Governor, Major Millman, entered the room and smiled nervously. The Chaplain included him in the conversation by a jovial nod. "Well, here we are, Millman — discussing the War and what not — I'd just been struck with an idea — "

Millman sat on the edge of the table and fidgeted. He was always apt to be upset by this last interview with a condemned prisoner, for he knew from experience how unpleasantly it could sometimes turn out. He felt almost grateful to Newcome for not being the kind of person who would make a hysterical scene. "Don't go," he muttered to the Chaplain.

The latter turned to David. "Well, don't you think it's what we ought to tell the youngster?"

David made a mild gesture of protest with his hands. "Oh no — don't tell him that — never tell him anything like that — please don't — "

"But why not? Is n't it something that might have happened but for —"

"Oh no, no —"

"But why not, man?"

David said quietly: "You see, I don't think I could ever kill anybody."

"But I 'm talking about *the War.*"

"I know. That 's what I mean. War *is* killing." Suddenly the little doctor's voice rose slightly. "How could I spend so many years fighting *for* life and then fight *against* it? Why do you expect me to undo everything I have ever done? How can you live and sleep while this is all happening? How *can* you? Governor — preacher — we 've put such a lot of trust in you two — why have you let things come to this? Why can't you save us from these crazy miseries? Why should we put up with you if you can't? What use are you? People only ask to live in peace and do their work — you can have all the noise and nonsense to yourselves! We don't ask miracles. But in God's name, have n't you learned *any-*

thing in two thousand years? We're not afraid of death, but we'll need to be afraid of life itself unless you fix things better in the future!"

David sank down in the chair with his head in his hands. He was exhausted. He so rarely talked to people like that — it was an effort that left him entirely spent. When he looked up he saw that both the Governor and the Chaplain had gone, and that a familiar face was across the table top. "Hello, George," he said, smiling.

"Good afternoon, sir. Duty again."

"You sound hoarse — or is it my ears?"

"Not your ears, sir — my throat. I've a bit of a cold."

"Well . . . it won't matter much if I catch it from you, will it?"

"Ha, ha . . . that's a good one . . . glad you're feeling cheerful. When I first come in, sir, and saw you sittin' with your head down, I thought you was takin' on."

"Taking on?"

"Worritin', sir. They do, you know, most of 'em, when it gets as near as this. But as I 've said to all my mates, sir, I do believe the little doctor won't bat an eyelid."

"Do they call me the little doctor?"

"Yes, sir — some of 'em bein' Calderbury men for years, same as yourself. They like you, sir."

"Do they? Well, I like them, too. I love them."

"Well, sir, no harm in that, I 'm sure. Would you like a cup of tea?"

"Thanks, George. . . . Oh — and George — about to-morrow morning — it 's all over pretty quickly, I imagine?"

"Oh, bless you, yes, sir — nothing to worry about. Won't take more than a minute from the time you step out of here. No waitin'."

Crossing the graveled yard, the Governor and the Chaplain paced with many undertones and shoulder shruggings.

"Quite startled me, the way he suddenly

launched out. What had he got against us, anyway?"

"Damned if I know, Millman. I suppose it's as I've said all along — the fellow's pretty well off his head."

"Well, well, I'll be glad when it's over — I hate these affairs. . . ."

In the morning a light drizzle was falling, and David, after a night no more troubled than many previous nights, rose before dawn and watched a simple greyness invade the sky. Through the barred window he could soon see the prison wall, a long horizon of granite, with but two interruptions, the towers of the Cathedral, ghostly through the rain. Over the roofs there came the steady chimes, by long association more a part than a breaking of the silence; the first real sound began at seven, when the early morning train arrived from Marsland with the newspapers. David heard it steaming and clanking into the station. Only a whisper from afar; but it was the voice of Calderbury each morning, and David heard it as a friend's.

We live in a town for years and all its voices come to us so casually and with such small effort that we hardly know them till we are about to leave, and then, into our regret comes some little thing, the rattle of a cart over cobblestones, an old cracked bell in a church tower, the shout of a boy selling newspapers; and we can answer with nothing but our love. David was leaving Calderbury that morning. He knew it, and his heart was full of love for the little town and for its people. And he remembered, as often happens on the last, the first day he had seen it — Jessie pointing across the water meadows from the train window — "There you are, David — that's Calderbury. See the Cathedral? No, no, not *there,* stupid — that's the electricity works. *There!*" And he remembered, smiling to himself, that habit Jessie had always had — of seeing something herself and expecting other people to see it instantly, on a mere nod. That was one of the things

he had had to put up with; but he had always
respected her, and people did n't realize how
shocked, as well as puzzled, he had been when
. . . But it was all such a long time ago now,
nearly three months. Questions — answers —
"Now, doctor, would you mind telling us. . . .
I put it to you, Dr. Newcome. . . . But surely,
doctor. . . . Come now, doctor, you really
must explain. . . . *Don't lie to us, Newcome. . . .*"

"I don't lie, my friends, I can't help it if the
truth does n't sound true. Perhaps the truth
is always strange. They say my boy Gerald
never tells the truth — but he does, sometimes,
often, only people don't believe him. Truth
is what is believed — a lie is what is disbelieved
— how's that for a pair of definitions? I
don't much care for them, but the world does.
Let me tell the truth just once before I die.
I call it love. . . ."

The two warders got up (they had not un-
dressed) when they saw him standing by the
window, and George bade him good-morning.

213

"Good morning, George. Don't bother. It's still very early. I'm all right."

"What would you like, sir? Coffee? Tea?"

"It matters so much, does n't it? Let's say tea."

So the tea was made, and David drank two cups. He did not eat anything, but he smoked his pipe for a while. He felt — well, not exactly nervous, but a little excited, as when, during student days, he had made his first knife cut into living flesh.

Presently a stranger entered the room and pinioned his arms with a leather strap; he submitted to this without word or murmur. Then he saw the Governor and the Chaplain standing by. "Good morning," he said, and smiled at them.

Across the graveled yard there was a small building whose use he had not realized before, but it was not far to walk to it, through the rain and in the chilly morning air. Then, obeying the gestures of the stranger, he stood on a little platform with his head under a wooden beam. A white hood was put over his head. Just at that moment he heard George cough, and then (they were his last words) he said, in a voice that came muffled through the hood: "That cold of yours is n't any better, George." The noose slipped over his head and he suddenly remembered Leni, and her little crushed smile, and that she too, at the same moment in Midchester. . . . Come with me, go with me, I don't know where, but there are a few of us, we make a good company already, we carry love in our hearts, we are not alone. . . .

The lever moved, and the little doctor's body fell into the pit, from which, later in the day, it was retrieved for burial inside the prison precincts.

EPILOGUE

I WAS in Calderbury a few weeks ago and as I passed the corner of Shawgate I noticed that workmen were pulling down the old house. One of the inside walls was exposed to view, and on it hung what seemed, at a distance, to be a picture that no one had bothered about. Even while I watched, it was taken down by a workman, and later I saw it handed over to someone in the little crowd which, in days of unemployment, and especially in a place like Calderbury, always collects round any scene of activity.

He was a young man of perhaps thirty, slim and not at all robust-looking, attractive in an eager, ascetic way, and rather shy in manner as

216

he took the picture, wrapped it in a newspaper he carried, and tried to slip away unobserved. But the crowd turned their slow curious eyes on him and someone called out: "Let's have a look, mister." At that he almost bolted, crossing the road at a tangent, and colliding with me on the opposite curb. The picture fell with a tinkle, and I made some apologetic remark, though it was really his own fault. He answered: "Oh, it doesn't matter — the glass was smashed already."

With a tidy gesture which I liked in him he began to kick the glass fragments into the gutter, away from danger to passing traffic. I joined him in this usefulness, and while we were both busy I said: "I don't know what sort of treasure you've got, but I suppose you know who used to live in that house they're pulling down."

"Oh, yes," he answered. "The little doctor. Did you know him?"

"Fairly well. I liked him. He cured me of asthma."

He laughed. "Well, that's certainly a good reason for liking him. I wonder if mine is as good. He brought me into the world."

We walked along some way in silence, wondering perhaps whether each was inclined for the other's company. Presently he said: "I suppose you remember the case?"

"You mean the — the Calderbury case?"

"Is that what you call it? I didn't realize it was quite so famous. I've been abroad a long time."

"But you're a native of Calderbury?"

"I left when I was nine. America — journalism — various things. I write poems — occasionally."

He said that in a nervous and rather truculent way.

"It's a pleasant diversion," I replied, "apart from any value in the poems."

He laughed enough for me to realize that I had said the right thing. "Come into my hotel and have a drink," he invited.

We went in and stood by the counter in the cool bar of the "Greyhound." There was no one about except Brierley, the landlord. He served our drinks and disappeared behind the glass screen. "Now that's the fellow," I said, "who really *could* tell you something about the Calderbury case. He was foreman of the jury."

"Don't ask him, please. I 've read all the newspaper reports — I 'm not specially interested in the police-court angle. I suppose it was a fair trial as trials go."

"Maybe," I answered. "There was a lot of circumstantial evidence, and I daresay many men have been hanged on less. And then, of course, there was a certain amount of political feeling about the girl, — German, you remember, — and it was the first autumn of the War. We all believed she was a spy. That did n't come up at the trial, — naturally, — but people like Brierley could n't help but be affected by it. The judge, I thought, was a shade too severe in his summing up — maybe *he* was affected too.   War fever is an insidious disease."

"You take an interest in the case?"

"I suppose I do — though only in a non-technical way.   I gather that *you 're* interested too?"

He smiled.   "Did n't I tell you he brought me into the world?"

"He did that to a good many young people you can see around the streets of Calderbury."

"Yes, of course.   But I did n't mean it in quite that sense.   You see . . . I 'm his son."

I looked at him then, incredulous for the moment, then in sudden silence as I remembered Gerald.   The little boy who cried and screamed and told lies and had nervous fits and whom nobody could control.   He seemed embarrassed at having had to explain his identity and went on: —

"I suppose you feel now you can't discuss the case any more with me?"

"Oh, *I* don't mind.   It 's more a question of whether you 'll want to discuss it with me when

EPILOGUE

you know who *I* am." I told him then my
name, adding: "I think we met — years ago.
At children's parties."

He nodded with a heightening of what
seemed a purely abstract interest. "Yes, I remember. And after that you were the star
witness for the prosecution."

"Don't hold that against me. I was too
young to know what it was all about."

"Do you mean you no longer believe he
was guilty?"

He shot the question at me so abruptly that
its awkwardness came as a challenge.

"Will you take my word if I answer that I
really don't know?"

He smiled. "Why, surely. . . . What
about another drink?"

"I think it's my turn," I said, calling for
Brierley.

When we were left alone again I went on:
"The evidence I gave was true enough, as far
as it went."

"Yes, of course. I never doubted it. You

221

saw my mother going into the house at a certain time, and you saw the other two leaving the house at a certain time. Ample opportunity. And a surgery full of poison. Logic. What more could you ask? Especially after the letter he'd written to the girl."

"Yes, it all pointed one way."

"And it all pointed wrong."

"Really?" (What else could one say? Well, there was one thing I could repeat.) "I must admit that if I'd known what use was going to be made of my evidence I'd have kept it to myself."

"But why?"

"Because I always liked the little doctor."

"Yet you don't feel certain that he wasn't guilty?"

"I don't feel certain of anything. How can I? Something mysterious and terrible happened over twenty years ago when I was a boy — why expect *me* to fix blame? Maybe the court was right, maybe not. The thing looked possible — more than that — even *probable*.

After all, we do know that murder is something that men will commit for love."

"So you think he was infatuated?"

"Call it that if you like the word."

"I don't, particularly. 'Love' is better."

"That's the word *I* used."

"Maybe they mean the same."

"Maybe."

"Do you think you understood my father?"

"Well, hardly — how could I? I was only a boy."

"There was something boyish in him. Childlike, almost. I once wrote a poem about him — perhaps I can remember it." He paused a moment and then recited, rather well:

> "Both youth and age were his
>   With no more change of scene
> Than from the blue of mountains
>   Down to the level green.

> "And in that blue-green land
>   Where English sons were bred,
> He knew the dead were living
>   And saw the living dead."

I said: "I rather like that. And I think I understand what you're driving at."

"The thing I'm driving at is that he wasn't guilty."

"Maybe not."

"*She* wasn't, either."

"You think not?"

"My God, I'm not telling you what I think — I'm giving you facts."

It seemed to me that I couldn't go on arguing with him. I said nothing, leaving him, if he chose, to continue. After an interval he said: "You see . . . I was in the house myself that night."

"*Really?*" (Again, what else could one say?) "How was that?"

"Simple enough. I'd been quartered with an aunt and uncle who lived at the other end of the town. I was lonely and miserable with them — or rather, I should say, I was lonely and miserable without my father. Just a prisoner in an enormous shabby vicarage. That evening — you remember it was the evening

224

war was declared — everyone was so excited by the news that I had my first chance to escape. I took it. I ran across the town, aiming for home. I climbed over the garden wall from the side footpath. Nobody saw me or would have cared much if they had. I thought the house was empty. I went to the surgery. It was always fun there, but that afternoon more than usual, because — well, because a cupboard usually kept locked was half open."

"Ah yes, I remember the evidence about that."

"So I had a nice game with some bottles, taking the corks out and sniffing. Damn lucky I didn't poison myself — or perhaps damned unlucky, when you come to think about it. Suddenly I heard footsteps in the hall. I was scared. I shut the cupboard as quick as I could and pushed away the bottles on a shelf where there were other bottles. I didn't want her to know I'd been touching anything."

"You knew who it was?"

"Oh yes, her walk was quite unmistakable. . . . Presently she came in and found me. She was very hot — it was a very hot day and she 'd been out in the sun. 'You here?' she began, but she did n't grumble as much as I 'd expected. I think she was tired. 'Where 's your father?' she asked. I said I did n't know. 'He 's never here when he 's wanted,' she said. Then she went to the shelf and took some pills out of a bottle. 'I 've got a bad head,' she said, 'and I want to lie down. Fetch a glass of water to my bedroom.' So I did, and that was how it happened. . . . All quite by accident, you see."

"Yes, I see."

"Don't you believe me?"

"May I say again — I don't really know. . . . At any rate, why did n't you tell all this to the court?"

"I never had a chance. I was only too glad to get away. . . . I 'd always been blamed for everything and I thought I should be again. . . . So I ran back to my uncle's house. They thought I was ill — one of my 'attacks,' they called them — I used to have bad nerves when I was a child."

"And you did n't tell *anybody* what had happened?"

"Well, they did n't tell *me* anything, either."

"What do you mean?"

"They never told me anything was wrong. It was weeks afterwards they said my parents had both gone away and I could n't see them. Years later I found out what had really happened. It came — " he hesitated for the understatement — "as a considerable shock to me."

There was another long pause, during which I recollected as much as I could of Gerald's reputation as a child. In the little town there had gathered quite a sizable legend of his precocious unreliability. He "romanced," or, if you cared to use the less flattering word, he told the most astounding lies. He would (in the days when I had met him once or twice at children's parties) assure people that he had

seen an elephant in Shawgate, or a collision
between two steam rollers going at full speed,
or a man with three noses. And once, I remember, he told a few of us very solemnly
that his father had bought a deathbed. How
he had picked up the word we could only guess,
but it was clear that in his mind a deathbed
was a particular kind of bed that one went to a
furniture shop to buy; so that was what he told
us, as calmly as you please. We thought it
amusing that his own childish ignorance should
so completely prove him a liar.

Thinking of all this, I said: "Well, it's a
pity you didn't tell the story when it might
have done some good."

"Yes, but I shouldn't have been believed.
At least, I very much doubt it. Nobody ever
believed me. Why, *you* don't even believe me
now. *Do* you? Honestly?"

"May I say — for the third time — I simply
don't know *what* to believe."

"I don't blame you. We none of us know
much about what really happens. Or has hap-

pened. The real truth is often hidden — perhaps because it's a dark truth. . . . It seems to me that we're all children of the dead — the dead who should n't have died — the dead who were put to death. . . . And they wait with us all the time, hoping we'll understand and learn something, but we don't, and we can't do anything about it. . . . Is all that too mystical for you?"

"I don't quite know what you mean."

He laughed as he answered: "Why should you? To hell with you, anyway. That's how you make me feel."

I smiled, liking him a little. After a short silence I said: "I'm interested in the girl — the German girl."

"Why?"

"I liked the look of her. I think I saw her once — before I saw her in the court. There used to be a motor bus that made journeys between the foot of Shawgate and Lissington Hill — the seats faced each other and one day I sat opposite someone I could n't help staring at.   Afterwards, when I described her to others, they said she must have been 'the foreign girl who works at the little doctor's.' So maybe she was. She wore a brown coat and a black fur hat like a fez. . . . But you knew her well, of course. Tell me what she was like."

His face lit with the beginnings of excitement. "She was . . . oh, I *can't* tell you. It's the nearest thing to heaven in my mind, — the only meaning heaven has, — that memory I have of her and of him. The little doctor — my little father. I used to watch them smile at each other. I used to go to sleep after they had touched me. They were *real* — and that's what's so hard to believe — that they were *ever* real. . . . Do you mind if we take a walk?"

"Good idea."

We went out into the streets of Calderbury, where it was growing dusk and lights were blinking from shops and houses; and far ahead, at the top of Shawgate, the towers of the Cathedral lifted insubstantially into the darkening east. Calderbury had survived, though how narrowly none could say. We passed the house where the little doctor had lived, and then, along Briargate, we passed the jail where the little doctor had died. That was being pulled down also — it was far too big and the site had grown valuable. I was still a little bothered by not knowing how much to believe of all that Gerald had told me, but I felt there must be a sort of truth in it, somewhere. "Well," I said, "you're probably right and there isn't a lot any of us can do."

"But there ought to be," he answered, so desperately that I was startled. "And, oh God, if only there were. . . ."